"I want

Lily stared at Tony, feeling her muscles melt.

"Tell me that you don't want me," he continued, "and all our future dealings will be strictly business."

Her skin was icy and hot all at once. "I can't tell you that."

He lowered his head again and closed his teeth around her bottom lip, then soothed the small pain with his tongue. "Then tell me you want me to make love to you."

She thought of lying to him, but then he leaned down and scraped his teeth against her neck. "You don't play fair," she said, a shiver running down her spine.

He smiled—a very slow smile that ruthlessly made use of his dimples. "I play to win. Tell me you want to make love with me."

She gave up trying to resist. Wrapping her arms around him, she conceded, "I want you. I really shouldn't, but I want you so much."

He let out a groan of triumph. "Good thing...because you've got me. You've had me from the moment you crawled into my bed."

Reaching down and pulling the string on his sweatpants, Lily said playfully, "Then let me see what I've got...."

Dear Reader,

I love writing WRONG BED books! What greater trouble can you plunge your heroine into than putting her in bed with the wrong man? And that's just the beginning of the fun!

Fresh from a success seminar in Tahiti, Lily McNeil is a new woman. The failures in her past are history. Not only has she shed twenty-five pounds, but she's also permanently erased the little black cloud that has hovered over her head since she was ten. And to prove to her skeptical family that the old Lily no longer exists, all she has to do is acquire Henry's Place, a small family-run hotel in Manhattan. So what if she has to lie to the owner to do it? No problem. The new Lily can handle it.

All Tony Romano wants is to keep his hotel running. When the sexy-voiced Lily McNeil offers her consulting services and promises that she can solve all his problems, he knows that she's lying through her teeth, but he figures he can handle her. He'll pick her brain, then send her packing. Tony's plan begins to unravel the moment he wakes up to find Lily sleeping in his bed. Then he wants to *handle* her, all right. And he does. Now all he has to do is figure out how to hold on to his hotel—and keep Lily in his bed permanently.

I hope you have as much fun reading Tony and Lily's story as I had writing it.

All the best,

Cara Summers

CARA SUMMERS

EARLY TO BED?

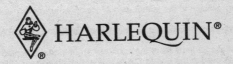

HARLEQUIN®

TORONTO • NEW YORK • LONDON
AMSTERDAM • PARIS • SYDNEY • HAMBURG
STOCKHOLM • ATHENS • TOKYO • MILAN • MADRID
PRAGUE • WARSAW • BUDAPEST • AUCKLAND

To Jane Frances Manor, my cousin and one of my biggest fans. Thanks for your unfailing praise and support! I love you, Janie.

ISBN 0-373-69170-X

EARLY TO BED?

Copyright © 2004 by Carolyn Hanlon.

This edition published by arrangement with Harlequin Books S.A.

® and TM are trademarks of the publisher. Trademarks indicated with ® are registered in the United States Patent and Trademark Office, the Canadian Trade Marks Office and in other countries.

Visit us at www.eHarlequin.com

Printed in U.S.A.

1

YOU CAN HAVE whatever you want.

Lily McNeil chanted the phrase silently, just as they'd taught her to do in the week-long success seminar she'd recently attended in Tahiti.

Your past does not have to equal your future.

That was phrase number two in her daily mantra. Somehow, the idea that she could transform herself into someone her family could respect had been easier to believe on a sunny beach with all those bright blue waves pounding on the shore.

Of course, the monsoon presently hammering Manhattan was having a debilitating effect on both her hairdo and her ego. And the fact that the taxi driver had dropped her off across the street from her hotel was a slight problem. Rain and wind lashed at her as she waited on the curb for the traffic to clear.

You live under a black cloud.

No. Tightening her grip on her rolling suitcase and her briefcase, Lily dashed across the street. She'd been ten when her stepbrother Jerry Langford-McNeil had first flung the black cloud taunt at her. For years after that, she'd carried the image around in her mind of a dark, rain-filled mist hovering over her wherever she went.

No more. No way. No how. Black clouds were in her past—and her past did not have to equal her future. In the past, her father had never approved of anything she'd ever done. But she was about to change all that.

True, her confidence had slipped a notch when the company plane had failed to pick her up in Tahiti. But she'd managed to charter another plane to bring her to New York. And she was here. Mission accomplished. Dripping, she pushed through the revolving doors of Henry's Place. Then she caught a glimpse of her reflection in the glass.

The old Lily was staring back at her—unfashionable, insecure, and overweight.

No. She was not that person anymore. Stopping short on the worn oriental carpet that ran up the stairs to the lobby, Lily squared her shoulders, drew in a deep breath and pictured herself the way she wanted to be. Visualization was the key to success. That's what the energetic motivational guru had preached on his island. Her five-hundred-dollar hairstyle might be a little under the weather. She risked a peek in the mirrored wall to her right and felt her stomach plummet. Okay—a lot under the weather. As for her clothes—she closed her eyes and suppressed a shudder. They could be replaced.

She risked another peek, just to make sure that the twenty-five pounds she'd struggled so hard to lose over the past six months hadn't somehow crept back onto her frame. They hadn't. Relief streamed through her. She might look like a drowned rat, but at least she was now a slim one.

Your past does not have to equal your future. Squaring her shoulders, Lily opened both eyes and faced herself in the mirror. She'd changed on the inside, and that was what was important. More important, her father,

J. R. McNeil of McNeil Enterprises, had given her a job and she had to prove to him that she could do it.

"Beware the Ides of March."

With a start, Lily whirled to see a tall ethereal-looking woman standing at the top of the short flight of stairs. She wore a gauzy caftan in faded shades of blue, and her slivery white hair flowed down over her shoulders. She might have been a witch sprung right off the pages of a Harry Potter book. But the voice didn't go with the rest of her. It had an "I don't take any crap" tone that sounded more like a five-star general's. The contrast aroused Lily's curiosity, but then she met the woman's eyes and felt a chill right through to her bones.

"Beware the Ides of March," the woman repeated.

Any mention of the Ides of March brought two memories to Lily's mind. First of all, the fifteenth of March was her birthday, and she'd just celebrated it two weeks ago. And anyone who'd studied Latin in school would recognize the warning that the soothsayer had given to Julius Caesar when he'd marched into Rome. Of course, the soothsayer's prophecy had been dead on. As if on cue, lightning flashed and a huge clap of thunder rattled the glass doors.

Lily jumped.

"Hurry!" Raising one jeweled hand, the witch beckoned to her. "Disaster is near."

Lily climbed the short flight of stairs to the lobby. If this was the way the hotel greeted its guests, it was no wonder that Henry's Place was in dire financial straits. And it had such potential. Its location within walking distance of the theater district as well as Central Park was prime.

Though her father had shown her the file on the hotel the Romano family had been running for almost fifty years, the picture that the lobby presented was worth much more than the thousand words of his report. Decaying was the word that came to mind. Why in the world was Anthony Romano, the family spokesperson, refusing to sell to McNeil Enterprises when they obviously couldn't take care of the place themselves?

In the end, the answer to that question wouldn't matter. During her week's stay at the hotel, her job, as her father described it, was to gather all the information she could to ensure that McNeil Enterprises' next offer would not be refused. *Find the weaknesses so we can exploit them.*

"Leave your bags here." The witch waved a hand at the mahogany reception desk that formed an L against one of the walls.

Lily immediately set down her suitcase and briefcase and followed the woman. She would have felt a lot better about the job her father had given her if she hadn't had to lie about why she'd really come to Henry's Place. She'd told Anthony Romano that she was heading up a new department at McNeil Enterprises that offered consulting services. She could provide him with an analysis that would allow him to revitalize the hotel. She was even supposed to offer him a financing plan. Of course, it would be a fake. Her real job was to ferret out information that would allow her father to force the sale.

The old Lily would have balked at the deception, and she would have described the job as spying. But the new Lily had to prove to her father and her step-family that she was fully capable of assuming a leadership position at McNeil Enterprises.

On the bright side, she might actually be doing the Romano family a favor. Their hotel looked as if it might not survive much longer in its present condition. As she followed the witch/soothsayer to a far corner of the lobby, she couldn't help noting the marble floors were chipped in some places, gouged in others. The carpets covering them, though they must have been charming in their heyday fifty years ago, were badly in need of repair. As for the furniture—the tiny, exquisitely carved settee creaked ominously when her soothsayer sank down on it.

It was only then that Lily noticed the white pillar candles and the crystal ball on the small table in front of the settee.

"Sit." The woman waved her to a chair across from her.

Still wondering how the five-star general's voice could come out of that fragile body, Lily did as she was told.

"Give me your hand."

Lily hesitated.

"Hurry. You don't have any time to waste. The future is yours to shape."

Lily stared at the woman. The words were such a close paraphrase of her motivational guru's words that she found herself extending her hand. As soon as the long slender fingers closed over hers and turned her palm up, she felt another chill move through her. For a moment, the lobby became so still that Lily could hear the wind whistling outside the doors as if it were searching for a way in.

"Right here is the problem." The woman traced a finger along her palm. "A line of deception. Today you begin a web of lies that could lead to great unhappiness for you and others."

For the second time in as many minutes, Lily felt her stomach sink. How could this woman know that she had come to Henry's Place on a spy mission? Had she failed before she'd even begun? Oh, that would make her stepmother and her stepbrother very happy.

"Why are you doing this?"

Why? That was a question she'd asked herself every day on that island retreat. But the answer always came back to the same thing. This was her one chance to win her father's approval.

"Look at how short the line is." The woman glanced up for a moment and met Lily's eyes. "You're not very good at deception."

Maybe not. The problem was that she hadn't been good at anything in her life. She hadn't been the son her father would have preferred. Two years ago, she hadn't been able to go through with a marriage that would have merged McNeil Enterprises with Fortescue Investments.

"Ah," the woman said. "This other line—right here—is your love line. You have a lover in your future—tall, dark, handsome."

Right. For the first time since she'd entered the hotel, Lily felt her tension ease. Finding a lover was standard patter for fortunetellers. The woman was obviously a hoax.

"Lovers from different worlds never have it easy. But if you have the courage to give yourself to him, he will love you for who you are," the woman said.

A fantasy, Lily thought, but she couldn't drag her gaze away from the older woman's. How could a stranger—someone she'd just met—know that having someone love her for herself was her deepest, most secret fantasy?

"Dame Vera, here you are. Sir Alistair and I were so worried when we couldn't find you."

Lily felt a little as if she were wrenching herself out of a trance, but she managed to tear her gaze away from the older woman's and shift it to the two people who were approaching. The young woman had dark hair, nearly black, that fell in a straight line to her shoulders. The name tag on her crisply ironed white shirt read Lucy. The man she'd called Sir Alistair was tall with finely chiseled aristocratic features that went with the wine-colored smoking jacket. Lily guessed his age to be somewhere between sixty and one hundred. He looked vaguely familiar—like an old friend she hadn't run into in years.

"You could hardly expect me to remain in my rooms. The bathroom was flooding." Turning to Lily, she murmured in a stage whisper, "Think *Titanic* an hour and a half into the movie."

"I fixed the leak temporarily," Lucy said. "Tony will see to it first thing in the morning. And of course, we'll have a cleaning crew in." Pausing, she sent an apologetic smile at Lily. "Dame Vera is one of our permanent residents, and she loves to tell fortunes."

Vera rose from the settee. "I don't tell fortunes. I see into the future. It's a gift that carries with it a great deal of responsibility. Disaster is near and the fate of Henry's Place hangs in the balance."

Dame Vera? The name had a memory tickling at the edge of her mind.

"You don't have to worry. You'll always have a home here," Lucy said in a soothing tone.

"A new owner might not see it that way."

Lily shifted her gaze away from Dame Vera's piercing stare in time to see shock appear on Lucy's face.

"Tony would never sell this place. He promised Uncle Henry that he would keep it. It's our family home—and yours, too."

"Time will tell," Dame Vera said, slipping back into her booming soothsayer voice. "In any case, it wasn't necessary to bother Sir Alistair."

"She didn't bother me, my dear," the man said. "I came over to see if—"

"You came over to check on me." Vera glared at him. "I don't need a keeper."

Sir Alistair. The name along with the British accent finally rang a little bell in the back of Lily's mind. Sir Alistair Brooks was a British film star she'd seen in a number of late-night movies. And Dame Vera? Lily peered more closely at her soothsayer.

"The day I get so forgetful that I can't find my way back to the rooms I've been leasing for more than half my life, you can book me a suite at Bellevue," Vera continued.

"I knocked on your door because one of your old movies is on the late show," Alistair said. "*Blithe Spirit.* Elvira was one of your greatest roles, and I have a nice bottle of Merlot."

Vera snorted. "What you have is a lecherous mind. And you know I prefer champagne."

"One of these days, you're going to agree to let me educate your palate."

Vera slipped a hand through his crooked arm. "I've been drinking champagne since—"

"I know, I know—since Sir Richard Harris drank it out of your slipper. Well, he's gone, but I'm still here. And I don't believe they have suites at Bellevue," he said as he led her toward the elevator.

"If that's your way of suggesting that I move in permanently with you, you can dream on."

"Always, my dear," Alistair replied.

Lily had to suppress the urge to applaud as the elevator doors slid shut on the couple.

"I hope she didn't bother you," Lucy said as she leaned down to pinch out the candles. "There was quite a leak in her suite, and I'm the only one on duty tonight."

"Don't worry about it," Lily said. "That's Sir Alistair Brooks, isn't it? The British film star?" Growing up in boarding schools, she'd clocked a lot of hours watching old movies while other kids were home for the holidays.

"Yes," Lucy answered, giving her a surprised look.

"And Dame Vera Darnel. I didn't put it all together until I saw them walk away. They appeared together in film versions of *Taming of the Shrew* and *A Midsummer Night's Dream*. I must have seen both of those at least twenty times. And about ten years ago they did a stint together on *Day by Day*." The daytime soap had been a favorite in the boarding school she'd gone to.

Lucy smiled at her. "Not many people recognize them anymore."

"They're guests here?"

"Permanent ones. Their suites occupy the eighth floor—right above the family suites on the seventh floor. They were my Uncle Henry's first guests, and the fact that they signed a ten-year lease fifty years ago gave him the financial security to open the hotel. They've been leasing here ever since."

"Is the leak a bad one?" Lily asked.

For the first time, worry replaced the smile in Lucy's eyes. "I'm sure that Tony can handle it. The plumbing has been acting up a bit more than usual lately. I'm sorry that I wasn't here to welcome you when you arrived."

"No problem," Lily said. But it occurred to her that she would have to include the incident with Dame Vera and the problem with the plumbing in her report to her father. Feeling guilty, she rose and followed the younger girl to the reception desk.

Once she was behind the counter, Lucy beamed a smile at Lily. "Why don't we start over? This is where I say, I'm Lucy Romano. Welcome to Henry's Place."

"I'm Lily McNeil and you must be Anthony Romano's sister?"

"Cousin," Lucy said. "But he's really more like a brother. I've lived here in the hotel all my life. Usually, I work in the kitchen, but all the men in the family are out tonight. My cousin Sam got married a month ago, and they're playing poker at his new place."

"I spoke with Anthony on the phone." Lily drew a credit card out of her purse. "I have an appointment to talk with him in the morning about renovating the hotel, and he made a reservation for me to stay here tonight as a guest."

Lucy's fingers flew over the keys of the computer.

"I'm so glad you have a reservation. We're booked solid. Thanks to the plumbing problem, there isn't a room to be had. Now..." Lucy leaned back in her chair. "All we have to do is wait for the slowest computer in the world. I keep telling Tony that he has to get a new system. All he says is that he's got it on the list."

While Lucy chattered away, Lily glanced around the lobby again. In her mind, she pictured it as it had been in its prime. It was really a crime to have let it deteriorate this way. At least when her father took it over, the lobby would be returned to its original beauty.

"Uh-oh," Lucy said with a frown.

"What?"

"I've pulled up your reservation, but there's a notation on it that it's been canceled."

"That's impossible," Lily said as she pushed away a vision of a little black cloud forming over her head. First a monsoon and now a canceled reservation. This was the kind of luck the old Lily had, and she was no longer that person. "Your cousin made it for me himself."

Lucy's frown deepened as she studied the screen in front of her. "He's also the one who canceled it. There's a notation that someone at McNeil Enterprises called this afternoon and said that your plans had changed."

Thoughts whirled through Lily's mind. Who would have called? Had her father changed his mind about the job he'd given her? Surely, he would have called her first to let her know. "There must have been some mix-up at the office. Why don't you just give me another room?"

Lucy met her eyes. "I don't have another room. I can

find you something at one of the other hotels in the city."

"Surely, you must have something." One thing Lily knew about the hotel business was that there were always rooms held back for just such an emergency. "Your cousin Anthony and I talked about how important it was that I stay here at Henry's Place. It's the only way that I can really get a feel for the place."

Lucy's brow knit. "I would have a room if it weren't for the plumbing. Dame Vera's wasn't the only room affected."

"I'll take anything," Lily said.

"Tell you what," Lucy said. "I do have a suite on the roof. My Uncle Henry lived there while he was alive, and it's only used by family." She swung out from behind the counter, picked up Lily's suitcase, and led the way to the elevator. "I'm sure that Tony would want me to put you up there. I know that he was looking forward to meeting with you."

As she followed the young girl, Lily let out the breath she was holding. In spite of Dame Vera's dire predictions, her past was not going to become her future.

"I'LL TAKE THREE." Tony placed his cards face down on the table and wished fervently that he could have discarded his entire hand. The grinning look that passed between his brothers as Sam dealt him new cards added salt to the wound.

"Don't get too smug," he warned his brothers. "My luck is going to turn. Dame Vera read my palm just before I left this evening."

"Did she give you a date on the turnaround?" Drew asked.

"Tonight sometime," Tony said. At least, he hoped it would be tonight.

Drew and Sam exchanged another look.

"I don't think we have anything to worry about yet," Sam said. "You haven't won a hand all night."

Though he wouldn't have said that he had a pessimistic nature, Tony viewed his current cards as symbolic of his luck in general lately. The hotel, his family's home, was threatening to fall down on his head. Literally. So far, he'd managed to keep the severity of the situation from his brothers. They didn't need the grief. They certainly didn't need to know that two big hotel conglomerates, McNeil Enterprises and Fortescue Investments were pressuring him to sell out. Not that he ever would—and certainly not to McNeil Enterprises. His father and J. R. McNeil had a history. That was all Tony knew, but it was bad enough for his dad to warn him never to trust anyone from the company.

Still, Tony would have liked to discuss the hotel's problems with someone. But Sam was a newlywed, and Drew had been working some tough undercover assignments at the precinct lately. The one person he might have confided in, his cousin Nick, was adjusting to fatherhood in Boston. He didn't need anything raining on his parade, either. Besides, running the hotel was Tony's job—the one his father had left him.

"I only need one," Drew said as he tossed his card on the table.

"And I'm good," Sam said.

That figured, Tony thought. Truth told, Sam's luck was on a roll. He was not only winning at poker tonight, but ever since he'd met and married A.J., his whole life had been on an upswing. The security company he worked for had made him a VP, and A.J. was expecting a baby in early summer.

"I'm in for twenty," Drew said, pushing chips into the center of the table.

"Big talk." Sam set a neat stack next to Drew's. "I'll see that and raise you thirty."

Drew added chips and the two men looked expectantly at Tony.

"You can always fold now," Sam said. "That way you can hold on to that pitiful pile of chips in front of you."

Tony turned to Drew. "That sounds like a bluff to me. I'll bet he's got squat."

"How much?" Drew asked.

"Ten bucks," Tony said.

Drew grinned. "You're on."

Sam shook his head sadly. "This is like taking money from a baby. You guys are no challenge at all."

Tony's smile spread slowly. "Those three cards you just dealt me could make me a full house."

Drew snorted. "Not with the string of luck you've been having."

"I told you. It's about to change," Tony said as he placed his hand over the cards and rubbed them gently against the table. They wouldn't give him a full house since he had an eight and nine in his hand. But they had to give him something. If there was one thing he believed in it was that a person's luck could change as quickly as the weather.

And Dame Vera's prediction had only reinforced his own personal feeling that his was certainly due for a change. The feeling had started a week ago on the day that Lily McNeil had contacted him to offer her consulting services.

She'd been the third person to contact him from McNeil Enterprises. First there'd been the invitation to lunch with J.R. Then there'd been the personal visit from the well-dressed and well-manicured Jerry Langford-McNeil. Not only had Lily been number three—Tony's lucky number—but he sensed something about her that was...different. Her father and stepbrother were smooth-talking sharks. His impression of Lily was that she was more of a goldfish. He gave the three cards on the table a rub.

Of course, he hadn't believed one word of the line of baloney she'd fed him over the phone. She claimed she was starting a new department for her company, and she wanted to help him get an affordable loan to make the improvements that he'd always wanted to make. Plus, she would offer him a free analysis and a plan to increase profits so that he could pay off the loan in record time.

Yeah, right. And then she'd probably have a bridge she'd want to sell him, too. No, it wasn't her too-good-to-be-true offer that had intrigued him. Her voice had caught his attention. Throaty and sexy, it had contrasted sharply with her brisk and businesslike presentation of her offer. And for some reason, it had made him think of hot, sweaty, all-night sex—the kind he'd fantasized about as an adolescent.

"Are you going to pick up those cards or not?" Sam asked.

"In a second." Tony continued to rub them gently against the table. He'd been looking forward to meeting Lily McNeil. Contrasts had always intrigued him. And when she'd laughed—

Hell, he'd really wanted to meet her—and not just to discuss business. He wanted to make her laugh again. And he wanted to watch her eyes light up when she did. He'd lost track of how long it had been since a woman had aroused his interest the way Lily McNeil had during their one phone conversation.

Then today, her office had called to cancel. She'd changed her mind about helping him, and she hadn't even had the courtesy to call in person. Tony drew the cards closer to him. "I'm definitely due for a change of luck."

"You could certainly use some at the hotel," Drew said. "Lucy was hauling buckets up to the eighth floor when I stopped in for a quick shower. The latest leak started there and flooded Dame Vera's apartment. When are you going to break down and get the plumbing replaced?"

"It's on the list," Tony said as he drew the first card toward him. Of course, the list was huge—a new computer system for reservations, a new stove in the kitchen, new carpeting for the lobby. But a leak on the top floor would have to be the priority. If it was allowed to continue, all the guestrooms below would be in danger. He managed a quick look at his watch. Eleven-thirty. Another half an hour and he'd make an excuse to leave.

"Now you've done it," Sam said to Drew. "He's going to make some excuse to leave now so he can check on that leak."

"Not until I win this hand, and the ten bucks that Drew will owe me when you turn over the squat you're holding." Tony pushed chips into the center of the table.

"You haven't even looked at your cards," Sam pointed out.

"Don't have to. Dame Vera told me my luck is about to change." He picked up the first card and bit back a grin. The queen of hearts was a good start. An omen, perhaps. Then he picked up the last two cards and filled in his straight. Leaning back in his chair, he kept his face blank and let his brothers up the bet.

2

LILY HAD NEVER SEEN ANYTHING quite like the penthouse suite before. It had been built on one half of the roof of the hotel, and it spread out on two levels, a lower one that served as a roomy sitting area and an upper level that contained a kitchen and dining space. The most spectacular part was the glass wall that framed a panoramic view of the Manhattan skyline. Even in the rain, the city was mesmerizing. In her mind, she pictured tables lined up against the glass, snowy white tablecloths, the gleam of silver.

"Perfect." There was no other word for it. Turning to Lucy, she said, "Why isn't this space being used? Why isn't it booked all the time?"

"We've never offered it to guests," Lucy explained as she stepped down into the sitting area. "My Uncle Henry built this place for Isabelle Sheridan, the woman he loved. They were a classic case of star-crossed lovers. She ran a very important investment company in Boston, and her family was socially prominent. They would have looked down on my uncle—to put it mildly. And running this hotel was his life. He could never have given it up and moved to Boston. She couldn't turn her back on her family and her company and move here."

"They never married?"

Lucy shook her head. "They used this place whenever they could for twenty years. Isn't that romantic?"

"Yes." Lily let her gaze move around the suite again. What would it be like to have someone love you enough to build a space like this? She noted the comfortable-looking sofas, the antiques, and the framed photos on tables and along a mantel. Curious, she joined Lucy on the lower level and picked up a large framed photo. Four handsome men, their arms linked around each others' shoulders, stared back at her.

You have a lover in your future—tall, dark... Even as Dame Vera's words slipped into her mind, Lily's gaze was drawn to the tallest of the four men, and she had the strangest sensation of...what? Surely not recognition. She'd never met any of the men in the picture. Still, there was something about the tall one...not merely his looks, she thought. All four of them would draw a woman's eyes. And it couldn't be merely the smile—because they were all grinning at her.

No. He was *not* the lover Dame Vera had been talking about. It was ridiculous to believe that the retired actress had any kind of power for seeing into the future. Besides, Lily McNeil wasn't in the market for a lover. She'd never had a talent for attracting men that way, and she didn't need any more failures right now. She had to focus on the job she'd come to do.

But she couldn't seem to drag her gaze away from the man. His smile made her feel that they were sharing some private joke. And she thought of her phone conversations with Anthony Romano. She'd felt a similar sense of connection then.

"Those are the Romano men," Lucy said. "Grace and I weren't allowed in that picture. That was the day that they won the basketball tournament with the Murphys, and the testosterone was running high. Whenever that happens, they get just a little chauvinistic." She swept a hand out. "And they don't think of this place as romantic at all. Tony and Nick think that Uncle Henry was a fool to settle for half a loaf. None of them liked Isabelle Sheridan. They thought she was a snob. But my sister Grace and I think it's great that she and my Uncle Henry found some way to be together. When I first saw the movie *Titanic*, I thought of my uncle—falling in love with someone out of his social class. Soooo romantic."

And potentially heartbreaking, Lily thought. It took a great deal of courage to reach out and grab that kind of love. A tiny shiver ran up her spine as she realized that she'd nearly echoed Dame Vera's words again. Even as she tried to shake off the thought, she realized that she was still staring at the tall man in the photo. She had to focus.

Setting the picture down, she forced herself to glance around the room again. It appeared that nothing had been changed since the two lovers had occupied it. "Does your family use this place often?"

"No," Lucy said and then she grinned. "Not until a year ago when my brother got married. Now he and his wife stay here when they visit from Boston. And Sam brought his wife, A.J., here one night—before they were married—and they got engaged the next day. My sister Grace thinks the place has the power to make true love happen."

"I was thinking it has the power to make the hotel a lot of money. With that view, this place could be turned into a restaurant that offers intimate fireside dining during the winter and al fresco dining during the summer months. It's a sin to let it go to waste like this."

"That's exactly what I've been telling Tony," Lucy said. "I even designed a menu."

When Lily glanced at her curiously, she hurried on. "The minute I graduate from college, I'm going to a culinary school. Tony lets me create specials for the restaurant, and he's incorporated several of them into the regular menu. But the family wants me to get a degree like Grace and my brother Nick did." She wrinkled her nose. "That way I'll have something to fall back on if being a chef doesn't work out. But I don't see the point. I've known what I wanted to be since I was ten."

"That's when I decided what I wanted to be too," Lily said.

"Really?"

"Yes." She hadn't let herself think of that day for a very long time.

"Did your family encourage you?" Lucy asked.

"No." It still hurt to recall what had happened when she'd worked up the nerve to march into her father's office to tell him. It had been one of the few times in the years after her mother's death when he'd worked at home. Her nanny had orders to keep her out in the garden, but she'd slipped away because she'd wanted so much to spend time with him. When she'd burst through the door of his office, he'd been deep in conversation with two clients. The moment he'd looked at her, she'd become all too aware of her mussed clothes and dirty knees, and she'd been swamped by the feelings of inadequacy that she always felt in her father's presence. Still, she'd managed to blurt out what she'd come to say. One day she wanted to be a partner in McNeil Enterprises. To this day, she wasn't sure what her father would have said to her if one of the other men in the room hadn't begun to chuckle. Then her father had joined him. Even now, fifteen years later, she could recall the hot flood of embarrassment and her father's words later when the clients had left and he'd lectured her. "You'll never be a success in business. You're far too impulsive—just like your mother was."

"When did your family start to take you seriously?" Lucy asked.

Lily dragged her thoughts back to the present and straightened her shoulders. "I'm still working on them."

When her father had reluctantly agreed to let her handle the "problem" at Henry's Place, the expressions on the faces of her family had been less than congratulatory. Shock and anger had flashed into her stepmother, Pamela's, eyes. And the usual mocking derision in Jerry's had been replaced by cool speculation.

At least no one had laughed. Once you'd been pegged as a failure, it was hard to change that image. But she was going to give it her best shot. Turning to Lucy, she said, "I'd like to see your menu in the morning."

"Really?"

Lily smiled. "Really."

Lucy gave her a quick, hard hug. "I'm so glad you've come to help us out. If anyone can convince Tony to turn this place into a restaurant, you can."

"I'll do my best," Lily found herself promising.

A soft buzz sounded, and Lucy glanced at the pager

she pulled from her belt. "I have to get back to the desk. There are fresh sheets on the bed—and I keep the fridge and pantry stocked for Nick and his wife." She began to back her way towards the door. "If there's anything you need, just phone down to the desk."

Lily managed to keep the smile on her face until Lucy was gone. Then she sank down onto the nearest chair. She felt like a slug. Lucy was looking on her as a savior, and she was a traitor. It had been a mistake to get the girl's hopes up. She should never have asked for the menu. It wouldn't do to get personally involved with any of the Romanos. If she didn't remember that, she was going to fail at what she'd come to do.

Closing her eyes, she pictured herself back on that white sandy beach in Tahiti and drew in a deep breath. All she had to do was keep the right perspective. She was not here to take Henry's Place away from the Romanos but to prove to her father and her stepbrother and stepmother that she was capable of taking her place in the company. If she didn't remember that, she was going to backslide into being the family misfit again.

With a sigh, Lily opened her eyes and moved toward the open door on the second level. She was tired. What she needed was a good night's sleep. Then her perspective would come back to her. Everything would be as clear as it had been on that beach in Tahiti. But the moment she stepped into the bedroom, her eyes widened. This time, it wasn't the view of the Manhattan skyline that drew her gaze. It was the huge bed, raised on a platform, that nearly filled the room. As she moved toward it, she was vaguely aware of a fireplace to her left, but she didn't take her eyes off the iron-frame bed.

It was definitely the kind to take a lover in. The thought had slipped into her mind the moment she'd run her hand over the smooth, satin coverlet. This time she couldn't blame Dame Vera entirely for the direction her thoughts had taken. The older woman might have planted the seed, but Lily had to admit that the idea of a lover had taken root in fertile ground.

It had been a long time since she'd had a man in her bed. For the past two years—ever since she'd broken her engagement with Giles Fortescue—she'd devoted herself entirely to making herself over—getting her MBA and apprenticing herself to a small but exclusive hotel chain in Europe. There hadn't been time for a man. And before that, there'd been Giles. She hadn't thought of him, hadn't wanted to think of him, in a very long time.

She could still picture him in her mind—the lean, tanned face, the blond, Viking good looks. He'd been thirty-three—ten years her senior. She'd been fresh out of college, twenty-five pounds heavier, and not used to the social whirl her stepmother had swept her into. Giles had taken her under his wing the moment she'd been introduced to him, and she'd fallen for him. He'd been so kind and attentive that she'd grown to believe that he'd fallen for her, too.

Suddenly she realized that it didn't hurt to think about Giles anymore. Slowly, she grinned. How ironic that the sight of a bed made for lovers would somehow set her free from the man her family had handpicked for her. Unfortunately, he'd also been a man who'd found her so fundamentally unattractive that for three months, he'd never attempted to do anything more than kiss her good night. When he had made love to her, the experience hadn't exactly rocked her world. Nor had it rocked his.

Afterward, he'd told her not to worry about it. He didn't really think of her in that way. Oh, he'd wanted to marry her because if he married J. R. McNeil's only daughter, then the merger between Fortescue International and McNeil Enterprises would rest on a foundation that would appease the boards of both companies.

It was then that she realized that her father and her stepmother had arranged the whole "courtship." By marching down the aisle, she and Giles would perform their duty to the new company. Then they could each go their separate ways. He, of course, would find other women to satisfy his needs. Meanwhile she would run his home and entertain for him while he worked to take his place at the helm of Fortescue-McNeil Inc. Of course, eventually, they would have to produce an heir.

Shuddering at the thought, Lily climbed up and settled herself on the foot of the bed. For the first time in two years, she was able to think of Giles and not feel that horrible wave of inadequacy that had swamped her for so long. Perhaps, the success seminar in Tahiti really was working. Or maybe, it was the bed—a bed where two star-crossed lovers had found happiness together for twenty years. A bed that represented real love, real passion.

Whatever it was, she felt relieved—no, she felt quite happy that Giles had never become her husband. She certainly couldn't imagine rolling around on this bed with the very proper and very staid Giles Fortescue. The image flashed into her mind then—bright and vivid—she was lying on the bed, her body entwined with the tall man she'd just seen in that photograph.

No. She frowned. That was not going to happen. She'd come here to do a job. And just because she'd finally freed herself of the black cloud that had been Giles Fortescue, that didn't mean that she wanted to jump into bed with someone else—especially one of the Romanos. That would lead to disaster.

She slid from the bed and walked quickly back into the main room to pick up her bag. She was going to stick strictly to business. And the first step was to take a shower, go to bed and get a good night's sleep.

Her past was not going to equal her future. She was going to get what she wanted.

TONY STARED at the chunk of plaster that had loosened itself from around the light fixture and fallen smack onto the middle of his bed. *Look on the bright side.* That was his father's credo, and Tony had adopted it as his own.

He lifted the chunk off the mattress and tested its weight before he tossed it into the air and caught it. Well, the bright side was that he'd been playing poker at Sam's when the pipes had given out in Dame Vera's suite. Otherwise, about ten pounds of damp plaster would have landed right on his... No, he really didn't want to dwell on where the chunk might have landed. But he figured that the straight he'd been dealt at Sam's had not only won him fifty bucks, it had also saved his family jewels.

Dame Vera had been right. His luck was definitely on the upswing. And it wasn't just the card game that had convinced him. He'd had a close encounter with a crazy driver on the way home from Sam's. The dark blue vehicle had come out of nowhere. He'd caught the movement out of the corner of his eye and raced for the curb just in time. The driver hadn't stopped, and Tony hadn't gotten a partial plate number to give to Drew, who was a cop.

Just then, the overhead light dimmed and another chunk plummeted to the mattress.

Tony sighed. Now, if his personal luck would just carry over to the problems at the hotel. Zach Murphy, who'd been patching the plumbing in the building for years, had predicted this particular scenario with the annoying regularity of a Greek chorus.

"Ton, mark my words. If you don't replace the pipes in that building, the whole eighth floor is going to fall on your head."

The damn thing about Greek choruses was that they were always right.

Tony surveyed his room, the one he'd occupied since he was ten, and wasn't sure whether to laugh or to cry. He'd made a promise to his father eight years ago to keep the hotel running. It was the only home he and his family had ever known. His brother Drew, his cousins Grace and Lucy, his Aunt Gina—they all still lived here. And over the years, the profits from the hotel had provided a college education for each member of the family. Now, he had to figure out a way to keep the roof from falling on their heads.

It wasn't in his nature to be a pessimist, but he didn't make a habit of lying to himself either. Henry's Place was in trouble. Though it was still operating in the black, he couldn't afford to close off any of the rooms because of plumbing problems. According to Lucy, the latest flood had moved from Dame Vera's suite down through the family's floor and on to four rooms on the sixth floor. They were all going to have to be repaired and repainted, and he was going to have to come up with the money for Zach Murphy to replace the pipes.

Lily McNeil had promised to help him with all of that. He'd planned to pick her brain while she tried to lead him down the garden path. Why had she canceled at the last minute? He didn't think for a minute that McNeil Enterprises had lost interest in Henry's Place.

First thing in the morning, he was going to call Ms. McNeil's office and find out why she'd canceled their meeting, and then—well, he'd just have to turn on the Romano charm.

Suddenly, a yawn overtook him, and Tony realized that he was deep down bone tired. Whatever his plans for the morning, what he needed right now was a dry bed to sleep in, and as much as he hated it, that meant going to the roof. He was stepping into the hallway when another hunk of plaster hit the bed. Wincing slightly, he closed the door firmly behind him and strode down the hall to the private elevator. The thing to remember was that his luck had changed. He punched the button for the penthouse apartment.

His first surprise came when the doors slid open and he saw that the room was ablaze with lights. Striding forward, he flipped lights off as he went. They'd even left the gas fireplace on. He'd have to speak with Lucy and Grace. They were the only ones in the family who came up here on a regular basis, but it wasn't like them to be so careless. He was heading for the table lamp next to the sofa when he saw her stretched out on the cushions, her hand tucked beneath one cheek.

There was a moment, one stunning moment, when he felt his mind empty. He could have sworn that time stood still—or was it merely his heart that had stopped? One thought filled his mind. *It's you.*

Then because the idea was so unprecedented, so ridiculous, he took a deep, steadying breath and moved closer. He was tired, the ceiling was probably still falling on his bed, and there was a stranger sleeping on the penthouse sofa. He studied her for a moment. Not sleeping beauty—he discarded the thought as soon as it slipped into his mind. Perhaps, it was the fact that one of her hands was curled into a tight fist. But something made him quite sure that this was no sleeping princess waiting for her prince to come. The reddish-gold curls fanned out on the pillow made him think of Goldilocks, a tough little housebreaker. He was nearly able to summon up a smile. Nearly, but not quite—maybe when his heart beat returned to normal. He took in the pale, almost translucent skin, the delicate features and the stubborn chin. Then he glanced at the curled fist again.

A fighter, he thought, and this time he did smile. She was wearing a plain tank top and worn gray sweatpants that looked as if she did more than sleep in them. The toned muscles in her arms added to the impression. Delicate and tough, he thought, intrigued by the contrast. And then he let his eyes linger on her legs. They were long, slender, and...

The desire that moved through him like a sharp, hot blade had him breathing a little sigh of relief. That was a response he could understand. And it was a lot more comfortable than the one he'd had when he'd first looked at her.

He wasn't going to think about that stab of recognition he'd felt because it was absurd. He'd never met this woman before. He didn't have to wonder how she'd gotten into the penthouse. Lucy had obviously let her in. She was probably some refugee from the flooding on the sixth floor.

Dragging his eyes from her, he swept his gaze around the area. A neat gray suit was draped over the chair near the fire—and he caught a glimpse of lace and satin spread nearby on a stool. She'd had no trouble making herself at home. Then bending down, he studied what she'd spread out on the table. There was a small notebook with a silver pen lying next to it and a series of sketches. He skimmed the neatly printed list on the open page of the notebook. *Repair the plumbing, renovate the lobby, turn the penthouse into a five-star restaurant—Henry's.*

Tony frowned as he picked up and examined each one of the sketches she'd drawn. If he was reading them correctly, they were of different floor plans for expanding the penthouse suite into a restaurant. And they were good. He glanced at her again. There wasn't a doubt in his mind that she was writing about his hotel.

Who in the hell was she?

He swept his gaze more carefully over the area again, noting the small suitcase and the leather briefcase. A niggling suspicion formed in his mind even as he reached to examine the tag. One glance confirmed it—this was Lily McNeil.

Sitting back on his heels, he studied her again as questions lined themselves up in his mind like so many toy soldiers. Why was she here? Or perhaps more specifically, why had she canceled her reservation and then changed her mind? Or had she planned to sneak into his hotel incognito and gather information without his knowledge?

He watched the play of the firelight over her features. So this was the owner of that voice. She wasn't exactly the way he had imagined her. Nor did she seem to fit the voice. Looking at her didn't make him think of hot, sweaty all-night sex. Instead, she made him think of the slow, thorough, take-your-time-and-savor kind.

His gaze shifted to her mouth, and he imagined her taste—not sweet, but tart at first. The sweetness would lie beneath. He wanted to explore that mouth, linger until he'd coaxed out all the flavors. He reached out to touch one of her curls. He could see the different colors, cool gold with a hint of fire here and there. He wanted to touch her—to run his hands over that skin. Even as the images formed in his mind, desire tightened in his center as if his body already knew what it would be like to feel her softness arching against him.

Muffling a sigh, Tony reined his wandering thoughts in and dropped the curl he was still rubbing between his fingers. Then because he couldn't help himself, he ran his finger lightly down her cheek to her chin before he dropped it to his side. She wasn't a sleeping beauty, he reminded himself—and he wasn't the prince meant to wake her up. This was Goldilocks, and the fictional girl who'd caused quite a bit of havoc in the bears' lives. It was his job to see that Ms. Lily McNeil didn't do that to the Romanos. The family was his responsibility, and he had to put them first.

She stirred, and her lips parted. Tony stilled. Once again he felt his mind empty, and then all he knew was an almost overpowering desire to fit his mouth to hers and throw caution to the winds. If she struggled, that would be the end of it. If she responded... He ruthlessly clamped down the images that poured into his mind. He couldn't. It wouldn't be fair to her. And it wouldn't be smart. He forced himself to rise and then switched off the lamp next to the couch.

He hadn't grown up in the hotel business without developing a canny instinct about people—and Lily McNeil was trouble, both professionally and personally. Getting involved with her would definitely not be smart. He let his gaze rest on her again. But it sure as hell would be fun. And when was the last time he'd let himself think of doing something just for the fun of it? Not since his father's death when he'd had to shoulder the responsibility of the hotel. Eons ago, it seemed.

Giving his head a quick shake, Tony made himself walk to the upper level and through the bedroom door. What he needed was a good night's sleep. Whoever the hell Lily McNeil was, he was going to need all of his wits about him. And he'd better keep his libido under control.

Just then, lightning flashed. He saw it split the sky, and the thunder clapped so loud, so close, that the windows rattled. A warning, he thought. A second later, the lights flickered and went out.

Definitely a warning, he thought as he made his way into the bedroom.

LILY FOUGHT HER WAY UP from a dream. She'd been with her lover. He'd touched her hair and her cheek. His fingers had been callused, arousing. She'd been so sure he was about to kiss her. In that moment when he'd seemed to hesitate, she'd wanted so badly to open her eyes, to reach out and cover his hand with hers, to draw him closer. But she'd been trapped in that paralysis between sleeping and waking. *Don't go.* She'd tried to say the words, but no sound had come out.

And then he'd moved away.

The sharp sting of rejection brought her fully to the surface, and the moment she opened her eyes, she realized the suite was pitch black. A glance at the windows told her that nearby buildings were dark, too. A power failure. Rain pelted the glass in an unrelenting rhythm. In the distance, a flash of lightning forked through the sky, followed by a rumble of thunder. The noise from the storm—that's what had pulled her out of her dream, not her lover walking away. The dull pain of failure still lingered from the dream. Ridiculous, she thought as she sat up. She was not going to let her fear of failure creep into her dreams, too.

After pushing herself up off the couch, she used the furniture to guide her as she made her way to the upper level. Failure was a part of her past, and she was going to make sure it did not seep into her future. She was going to go back to sleep in that bed made for lovers. Then she was going to conjure up her dream lover and make sure he didn't pull away.

Running her hand along the wall, she made it to the door she was sure opened into the bedroom. The darker shadow three feet in front of her had to be the bed. Once she reached it, she felt her way to the side near the windows where she recalled seeing the stepstool. There. Once her foot connected with it, she climbed up on the mattress and slipped beneath the covers.

A yawn overtook her as her head settled on the pillow. The bed was so warm, so welcoming, as if a lover was already there, waiting for her. Her lips curved in a smile. Dame Vera had promised her one, after all. So what if it was only one conjured by her mind? A dream lover didn't interfere with your life. Closing her eyes, she emptied her mind of everything, then concentrated on calling up a picture of her dream lover. Visualization. That was the key. She hadn't seen him too clearly in the dream, so he could be anything she wanted him to be.

Slowly, she brought his features into focus. A strong nose, Roman, she decided. And the cheekbones of a warrior. His mouth was masculine, but the whole effect would be softened by dimples that appeared only when he smiled. And then there were his eyes. They were the color of dark, forbidden chocolate. Irresistible. The warmth of the bed began to seep through her. As she felt herself begin to sink into sleep, her dream lover's features became even clearer in her mind. Her last thought before sleep overtook her was that she'd seen her dream lover somewhere before.

3

TONY DRIFTED somewhere in the twilight zone between waking and sleeping. The last thing he wanted to do was surface from the dream he was having. His Goldilocks was sleeping in his bed. And it felt just right.

She was nestled against him like a spoon, her back to his front. Each time he inhaled, her scent filled him. He would have recognized it anywhere. Spring flowers, the kind his mother had taken such care to grow in terra cotta pots on the roof.

With lazy pleasure, he slipped one hand beneath her to keep her near and ran the other down her from her shoulder to her thigh. The contrast of warm silky skin and more roughly textured cotton had a warm flame of desire moving through him. She shifted, pressing more closely against him, and the flame eased into a slow, searing burn.

He slipped his hand beneath thin cotton. She made a throaty sound of pleasure when he cupped her breast, another when he scraped his teeth against the nape of her neck. He'd dreamed before of touching her like this, but the sensations seemed sharper now. Her skin was soft as water, her waist so narrow. Hearing the quick hitch of her breath, he let his hand take the long, slow journey again. He felt his own need grow as he absorbed each separate layer of her response—the pounding of her heart, the warming of her skin when he pressed his palm against it, the tremor that moved through her when he finally slipped his hand beneath the waistband of her sweats. Then he used his mouth on the back of her neck again as he slipped a finger into her heat.

THE ORGASM MOVED THROUGH HER in one, hot, consuming wave, and Lily thought she just might die from the pleasure. Then before she could catch even one breath or gather up the strength to move, those strong, clever fingers began to move deep inside of her again. This time each sensation was sharper. She inhaled his scent—something darkly male. And the heat of his body—it burned hers like a brand at each and every contact point.

She'd never dreamed anything this clearly before. His teeth bit the back of her neck as his hand tightened on her breast. She could hear her heart beat, feel each pump of her blood as it accelerated the way a locomotive did when it hurled itself down a hill. His fingers moved relentlessly, and though she hadn't thought it possible, a huge pressure was beginning to build inside of her again.

Then he withdrew his hand.

"No." The word came out as a ragged moan and she twisted and rolled, desperate until she lay across him. *Visualize.* This was a dream, she reminded herself. A wonderful one. If she just pictured everything clearly enough, it wouldn't fade. Her dream lover couldn't leave.

She conjured up his face in her head again—the strong features, one by one. It was working. She could feel his body beneath her, all hard planes and angles, pressing into hers.

"I want you," she said.

"Touch me."

Lily wasn't sure who said the words. All she knew was that she had an overwhelming urge to explore him with her hands, to memorize him the way he'd memorized her. With her eyes still closed, she traced her fingers over his brows, down the sides of his face to the hard line of his jaw. Yes, he was just as she'd pictured him. As she brushed just the tips of her fingers over smooth, firm lips, the image in her mind wavered a little. Slowly, she lowered her mouth to his. The urge to taste him was so huge, so consuming. His lips were parted, just slightly, and his flavor seeped into her— dark and tempting. His mouth was so warm, so gentle. When her tongue moved against his, the taste grew richer. Lily felt herself melting, skin, muscle, bones.

She was on the border between sleep and wakefulness, but as his hands began to move on her again, she couldn't summon up the strength to open her eyes. Lean and firm, his hands weren't gentle this time. They were strong and hard, the fingers callused. Wherever they pressed, flames licked along her skin. Threading her fingers through his hair, she arched against him, urging him on as she poured herself into a kiss.

TONY FELT his reason slipping away. She was so responsive, so giving. So his.

His hands had taken on a will of their own, racing over her, taking, touching, claiming. His mouth too seemed out of his control. He had to devour her. Even as her taste filled him, he couldn't seem to get enough of it. Some part of his mind was telling him that this couldn't be a dream, the sensations were too sharp, too real, but he had no will to listen.

He'd wanted a woman before—but not with this intensity. He'd needed a woman before, but not with this desperation. Desire hammered at him with sharp, piercing blows as he dragged off her clothes.

More. He had to have more. In some part of his mind, he knew that his hands weren't gentle as they raced over her. Those soft curves beckoned to him, but he had no patience to linger. Even though her scent enveloped him, even though her taste filled him, he couldn't get enough. He had to have her. His blood was pounding in his head as he rolled her beneath him and thrust himself into her. But as he did, she wrapped herself around him and matched her movements to his so that the two of them were perfectly in synch, driving each other higher and higher. Then as pleasure shattered through him, they merged as one.

WHEN SANITY RETURNED, she was lying beneath him. He was sure he was crushing her, but he couldn't move except to tremble. His breath was coming in ragged gasps. And he couldn't think. A cold sliver of fear moved through him. The last thing he clearly remembered was asking her to touch him. When she had, his control had begun to stretch thin like a rubber band— until it had finally snapped.

The one thing he was pretty sure of was that what had just happened was too real to have been merely a dream. Slowly, he raised his head, opened his eyes, and confirmed his worst suspicion.

The woman lying beneath him was indeed his Goldilocks, and she was real. Had he hurt her? The thought gave him the strength to lever his weight off of her. "Are you okay?"

Her eyes opened, and he found himself looking into a deep sea of green. As he watched, they darkened and focused, then shut.

"Did I hurt you?" he asked.

She opened her eyes, raised a hand to his cheek and frowned. "You're real, aren't you?"

The husky sound of her voice had him hardening all over again. Later, he would find that amazing. Right now, the effect was dimmed by the fact that she was clearly not pleased.

He tried a smile. The Romano dimples had gotten him over rough ground before. "Last time I checked, I was."

She shut her eyes. "I thought—I thought I was dreaming." Then her eyes snapped open again and her gaze narrowed. "Just what are you doing in my bed?"

The haughty accusing tone had him biting back a grin. It wasn't everyone who could pull it off, especially when they were naked and still lying partly under you. He planted a quick kiss on her nose. "*My* bed," he corrected. "When I came in, you were sleeping on the couch. So I claim squatter's rights."

"This is my room," she said. "Lucy Romano gave it to me. Therefore, this is *my* bed."

"Remind me to thank Lucy," he murmured as he lowered his mouth to hers. He meant to merely drop a quick kiss, but the moment his lips brushed hers, he had to have just one more taste, and then he had to have more. There was such sweetness on the surface— rich, wild honey, and when he nipped on her bottom lip, the flavor deepened. He told himself that he would have pulled back if she'd shown any sign of resistance. But she didn't. When he finally did withdraw, he waited until she met his eyes. "This isn't a dream."

"No," she said.

"I want you again."

Her eyes remained steady on his. "I want you too. But..."

He nibbled kisses along her jawline. "But what?"

"We're strangers. We don't even know each other."

He met her eyes again. "Do you want me to stop?"

She tightened her arms around him. "No."

Even as he made a space for himself between her legs, he said, "Are you protected?"

"No. I—"

He dropped a quick kiss on her forehead. "Don't worry. I'll take care of it." But he had not taken care of it before. They'd have to talk about that later. Reaching into the drawer of the nightstand, he removed one of the foil packets that his father had kept there. Once he had sheathed himself, he pushed into her just a little.

"We're going to take it slow and easy this time," he said.

"Oh? We are?"

Surprise and delight filled him when he saw the light of challenge come to her eyes. He'd been right in his first assessment of her. She was a fighter, all right. "Slow and easy," he promised. "I'll just have to persuade you."

"We'll see about that," she said as she tightened her legs around him and drew him in.

When the battle was over, neither was sure who'd won.

SHE SLEPT LIKE A ROCK, Tony decided as he slipped out of the room. Pausing in the doorway, he glanced back at her. She hadn't moved since he'd awakened at the first light of dawn. Not even the running of the shower had disturbed her. She was still sleeping on her side with one hand tucked under her cheek, in much the same position that she'd been in when he'd first seen her on the couch last night.

Goldilocks looked quite at home in his bed, he thought. And just what in the hell was he going to do about that? Turning, he moved toward the kitchen. Perhaps, coffee would defog his brain. The cold shower hadn't. Heaven knew after the night they'd spent, he should be sated with her, but he'd barely made it out of bed without waking her to make love again.

That was more than enough to give him pause. He couldn't recall another woman who'd ever threatened his control the way she did. As he measured water and scooped coffee into the coffeemaker, he reviewed the problem.

His father's warning to beware of J. R. McNeil no doubt included his daughter, too.

So—bottom line and in a nutshell—he'd just spent the night sleeping with the enemy.

And in spite of the fact that it probably wasn't a very good move on his part, making love to Lily McNeil had felt very right. So right that he wanted to do it again—and soon.

On the bright side, what he knew about her so far made him believe that she had an honest streak in her that ran bone deep. During the night they'd spent together, she'd delivered on every promise that that

sexy, throaty voice had made. And then some. Her
lovemaking was honest, generous and incredible.

And he definitely wanted to repeat the experience.

As he reached for a mug, Tony sighed. Clearly, his
judgment on the matter of Lily McNeil was not totally
impartial and objective. And dammit, the contrasts
that he'd noticed so far about her just plain fascinated
him. He shifted his gaze to the living room where her
neat, classy clothes hung on the back of a chair. She
wore that during the day, then sweats and a tank top to
bed. Who was she really? Was she the corporate shark
or Goldilocks? Not that those two categories were mu-
tually exclusive.

As the coffeemaker made its last gasping sputter,
Tony reached for the carafe, filled a mug and took one
long swallow. He welcomed the heat that burned his
tongue and seared his throat. That along with the jolt of
caffeine should help him to come up with a plan.

Another point on the bright side—Dame Vera had
predicted that his luck was about to change. Normally,
he wouldn't have paid much attention to her reading
of his palm. He'd only let her do it to humor her. But
he'd been feeling the same thing for the past few days.
Ever since Lily had first called him, he'd had a feeling
that something was about to happen—and it would be
good, for a change.

He took a second swallow of his coffee, then grabbed
the carafe and refilled his mug to the brim. What had
Dame Vera's exact words been? He recalled that she'd
been gazing at his hand, tracing a line that started between his thumb and forefinger and ran crookedly to
his wrist. He took another sip of his coffee and concentrated hard.

"Luck is coming your way. If you have the courage to grab it, everything will change."

Or something to that effect. He'd had a lot on his mind and he'd been late for the poker game at Sam's when she'd waylaid him.

But right now, his gut instinct was telling him that Lily McNeil was connected to whatever bit of good fortune fate was offering him. And he'd grabbed her. Now all he had to do was hang on.

At the same time, the little voice of reason was trying to make itself heard at the back of his mind. "What if the change is a bad one? What if you end up losing Henry's Place?"

He was still frowning when he'd finished his second mug. Then he turned to a time-tested strategy, one that had never failed him when he needed to work through a problem—cooking. He didn't have any porridge, but he could fix his Goldilocks an omelette.

By the time he'd finished shredding cheese and dicing herbs, he had it pretty well figured out. Point one: If Lily was here to spy on Henry's Place for her father's company, two could play that game. The more inside information he had, the better he'd be able to handle her father when McNeil Enterprises made its next move.

Point two: On a personal level, he'd be able to find out just what it was about Lily McNeil that had his hormones regressing to his adolescent years. He cracked eggs into a bowl and began to whip them into a froth. Point three: He could pick her brain. He'd had Sam check into her background, and she'd spent the past two years working in a small but exclusive hotel chain in Europe. She could be his key to saving Henry's Place.

His plan was to keep in very close contact with Lily McNeil. All in all, he could see no downside to the situation.

Especially when he had it on good authority that his luck had changed.

LILY CAME AWAKE slowly. She could feel herself floating up to the surface, but she didn't open her eyes, not yet. She felt too good just where she was. Her muscles were relaxed, loose...and just a little sore? Her first thought was that she was still in Tahiti where she'd run on the sandy beach every day. She burrowed more deeply into her pillow, but in the end, it was her senses that betrayed her—the sunshine pricking at her eyelids, the smell of freshly brewed coffee, and the sound of someone singing. She opened one eye. The song was familiar—an old Beatles song. The voice was decidedly male—and he was singing off key.

Lily shot straight up in bed and opened the other eye. Any hope that she was still in Tahiti vanished the moment she saw the New York City skyscrapers through the glass wall to her left. Memory came flooding back. She was in Manhattan in Henry's Place, and she'd just spent the night in a bed made for lovers. Correction. She'd just spent the night having crazy, wild and thoroughly incredible sex with a complete stranger in a bed made for lovers.

Covering her face with her hands, she sank back against the pillows and groaned.

"I guess you're not a morning person."

She felt her stomach plummet as she spread her fingers and peered through them. Yep. There was her dream lover in the flesh—just as she'd conjured him up. She narrowed her eyes and spread her fingers a little wider. Only perhaps, she'd had a little assistance with her visualization. Her stomach sank even further as she recognized the man standing at the foot of the bed as the tall man in the photograph she'd picked up in the living room. He was one of the Romanos.

"Try some of this." He smiled as he set a tray in front of her. She dropped her hands from her face and forced herself to look at the tray. The omelette was fluffy, the toast crisp and the coffee smelled heavenly. But she could smell him above it—that distinctive scent that was his alone. And it was making her melt again. "I'm sorry. I don't eat breakfast."

"You don't eat breakfast? It's the most important meal of the day."

The genuine shock in his tone had her glancing up. "I run first thing in the morning. All that food will slow me down. I might even get a cramp." She reached for the mug of coffee.

"Careful. It's hot."

She sipped cautiously, closed her eyes and drew a deep breath. Then she took two more swallows before she opened her eyes and lifted her gaze again to meet his. She cleared her throat. "Maybe we ought to introduce ourselves."

He smiled and held out his hand. "I'm Tony Romano."

"No." She set the coffee down so hard that it would have spilled if he hadn't steadied the mug. "You can't be."

"I could show you my driver's license."

In her mind, Lily pictured the black cloud she thought she'd escaped from settling over her head like a permanent lid. Dame Vera's words came back to her. *Disaster lies ahead.* Not that she had to worry about that anymore. The disaster had arrived in the flesh, and he was standing right beside her bed.

She was just going to have to deal with it. "That won't be necessary. I believe you." She cleared her throat again. "I'm Lily McNeil."

"I know."

She stared at him. "You know who I am? How?"

"When I walked in last night and saw you sleeping on the couch, my first thought was that you were Goldilocks. And then I saw the tag on your suitcase."

"You snooped?"

"The tag was out in plain sight. Tell me you wouldn't have done the same."

He was right. She was being ridiculous. She folded her hands tightly together in front of her. What would her success guru do in a case like this? Focus and visualize. The problem was she was finding it hard to picture anyone in her mind but Tony.

"Should I apologize?" Tony asked.

Steeling herself, she met his eyes again. "No."

"For anything, I mean. I wasn't exactly gentle with you."

She felt the heat rise in her cheeks as she recalled exactly how forceful he'd been. "You don't have anything to apologize for. Do I?"

She saw surprise in his eyes. "No. But you regret what happened last night, don't you?"

"I should, but I don't. I—" She raised both hands

and then dropped them. "I just wish we hadn't started out that way."

He took one of her hands and raised it to his lips. "I'll have to work on my technique."

"No." She read the intent clearly in his eyes and pulled her hand away. "Your technique is fine. It's great."

"I could try for exquisite."

She laughed then, and when he sat down on the bed and reached for her, she found it took a great deal of effort to raise a hand to stop him. "No. I can't. This isn't the way we should have started out. And it's not the way I mean to go on." She drew in a deep breath and let it out.

"You're telling me this was a one-night stand and it's over?"

"I don't see the need to put it that way."

"What happened to the old rule of three strikes and you're out?"

Lily stared at him. He was sitting on the other side of the breakfast tray he'd prepared for her—bronze skin, chocolate-colored eyes, and a body that ancient artists had trapped countless time in bronze or marble. And he was trying to convince her to make love with him again. All she had to do was reach out and—it took all her strength to summon up the faces of those who didn't believe that she could handle this job for McNeil Enterprises—her father, her stepbrother, her stepmother. "We're not talking about baseball here."

"True." He picked up a fork and sliced into the omelette. "Here, try a bite of this. Maybe my cooking will change your mind."

"No." She noticed that the "no" was easier to say

this time. The focusing was working. "I'm on a diet. And you're not going to change my mind."

"Why are you on a diet? You're perfect."

The look of complete amazement on his face had a little ribbon of warmth unwinding through her. She couldn't remember anyone ever describing her as even close to perfect. Focus, she reminded herself.

"I just lost twenty-five pounds, and I'm not gaining it back." She glanced at her watch. "Which reminds me, I have to run. What floor is your health club on?"

He was studying her and a small frown had appeared on his brow. "It's on the renovation list."

It was her turn to be shocked. "Where do you send your guests if they want to use a treadmill or work out?"

Tony ran a hand through his hair. "We don't."

"You should at least have a route mapped out for them so that they can run on the street. I'll take care of it for you." She lifted the tray and handed it to him. "Now, if you'll just let me get dressed for my run..."

Tony set the tray on the nightstand. "You're not running on the street alone. Wait until noon, and I can go with you."

"I don't need—"

He took her hand and this time he held it firmly enough that she couldn't pull it away without a struggle. "One favor. That's all I'm asking. Surely, after using me for pleasure and then dumping me, you owe me that."

She tried to keep her mind off the heat that was spreading through her just because he was holding her hand. Focus, she told herself. "Okay. One favor—I'll wait and you can run with me at noon."

"Deal." He smiled at her, and she felt her heart skip. As if those chocolate eyes weren't lethal enough, the man had killer dimples.

Focus. "And we're going to forget that last night ever happened. From now on, our relationship is strictly business."

Grinning, Tony shook his head. "No deal on that one. First of all, I don't believe in one-night stands. And right now, I want to make love to you so badly, it hurts."

She hurt too, Lily realized. And she could ease the pain by simply reaching out and— "No."

"Okay." Tony raised both hands, palms out. "You win. We'll play it your way for now."

"Good." It was relief she was feeling, not disappointment. Lily was almost sure of it.

Then in a move so quick she didn't even see it coming, he kissed her. It was a quick meeting of lips, friendly almost. But the arrow of heat it shot through her system was nearly lethal. Worse than that, it was enough to make her remember and yearn.

"It *was* good," he said as he drew back. "You remember that. I'm a patient man, so we'll take it slow and easy. I'm going to enjoy convincing you to change your mind."

Lily watched as he rose, picked up the tray and moved out of the room. Only then did she let out the breath she was holding. As she heard him start to sing again, she reminded herself to focus. *You can have whatever you want.*

And she wasn't supposed to want Tony Romano!

4

THE MOMENT THE ELEVATOR DOORS slid open, Tony knew he was in trouble. The lobby was occupied by far too many people for 8:00 a.m. on a Thursday morning. Dame Vera was already ensconced on her favorite settee overlooking the entrance. Sir Alistair Brooks sat a short distance away, his attention focused on *The London Times*. It was rare for either of them to appear in the lobby before noon. Dame Vera had tea in front of her instead of her crystal ball. That was good news. But the fact that his brothers were seated at a table in the lobby bar huddled with Murphy was not. Murphy was here to give him an estimate for the latest plumbing disaster, and Tony didn't like it one bit that Sam and Drew had decided to drop by for the meeting. Both of them should have been on their way to work by this hour.

Shoving down a quick spurt of anger, he strode toward them. He would have a word with Murphy. The hotel had always been his responsibility. Whatever the problem with the plumbing was, he'd handle it, and he didn't want his brothers involved. He was halfway across the lobby when Dame Vera's voice stopped him.

"May I have a word, Anthony?"

It was impossible to ignore a voice that had been trained to reach second and third balconies. Turning, Tony smiled. "I heard you had a leak last night."

"Leak?" she boomed. "They could have filmed *Titanic the Sequel* in my sitting room."

Alistair lowered his paper far enough to send Tony a sympathetic glance.

"Sit." Dame Vera pointed to the chair across the table from her. Once he seated himself, she leaned toward him and spoke in a stage whisper. "Disaster is near."

"Come and gone," he assured her. "Murphy will have your pipes mended today."

She waved a hand. "I'm not talking about the plumbing. This is much more serious. I had a dream last night."

Tony raised his hands, palms out. "I don't think I want to hear this."

This earned him an admiring look from Alistair.

"Nonsense," Dame Vera said.

"You promised my luck would change, and I believe it has."

She studied him for a moment, her eyes bright and shrewd. This time she spoke in a tone that only he could hear. "You've already met her, I see."

"Met who?"

Her eyes narrowed. "The woman who is going to change your life."

With a smile, Tony reached for her hand and raised it to his lips. "I met you years ago."

She threw back her head and laughed. The rich, throaty sound filled the room. But when he would have released her hand, she held tight. Her smile faded and she spoke in a low tone. "Beware the Ides of March."

Something in her voice had Tony's smile fading, too.

"It's March twenty-ninth. The Ides of March are over for this year."

"But the seeds of disaster were planted then and now it is near. Be very careful."

"I will." Tony gave her hand a squeeze before releasing it and tried to ignore the sliver of ice that ran up his spine as he headed towards the table where his brothers sat. There were some days when he suspected that Dame Vera might truly have a psychic gift. Not that he needed a psychic to tell him that by sleeping with Lily McNeil, he was taking risks both professionally and personally. However, he'd crossed that bridge, and now he'd have to handle it—just as he was going to have to handle his family.

As he settled himself in the chair next to Murphy, he quickly scanned the lobby again. Alistair had joined Dame Vera and Lucy was behind the desk handling a check-in. With Grace studying all the time for her law school classes, Lucy was taking on more of her hours. He had to think of hiring someone. Then turning his attention to his brothers, he smiled. "If you're here to win your money back, I'm afraid I'm booked solid today."

"We don't want your money," Drew said. "We want the truth about what's going on here."

"Nothing's going on," Tony said, "except the usual."

"You can stop with the line of bull," Sam said shortly as he filled a cup and passed it to Tony. "Dame Vera called me at the crack of dawn. A.J. took the message—and it was something about the Ides of March, disaster being imminent, and a woman who was going to change your life. A.J. was concerned enough that I called Drew to check it out.''

''Dame Vera called me with the same message. Who's the woman?''

Ignoring Drew's question, Tony said, ''If you've called this little meeting because of something that Dame Vera said, you can both relax. She also told me that my luck has changed. And I proved that last night.''

''Well, you're going to need all the good luck you can get, big brother,'' Sam said. ''Because according to Murphy here, we've got big trouble.''

''Plumbing repairs are part of the day-to-day story of running a hotel,'' Tony said.

''Tell him, Murphy,'' Sam said.

''The leak in Dame Vera's room wasn't caused by the general deterioration of your pipes,'' Murphy said. ''Someone cut them, not only in her bathroom, but in the kitchen and guest baths as well. That's why the water damage is so extensive on the floor below. They knew what they were doing.''

''Cut them? How?'' Tony asked.

''I've been thinking about that,'' Sam said. ''This is a family hotel, and the security is pretty lax.'' He raised a hand. ''That's not a criticism. But an employee or even any guest who stayed for a few days would be able to figure out the routine. Dame Vera likes to come down to the lobby at regular times—for a late breakfast and again for high tea in the afternoon. Someone with the proper motivation could also easily discover when the maid services her suite. It wouldn't take much to get in there.''

"But why?" Tony asked. "Why would someone deliberately sabotage the plumbing?"

Drew leaned forward. "That's what we want to know, bro. What haven't you told us?"

Tony looked from Drew to Sam. "You don't have to worry about this. The hotel is my responsibility."

"It's your albatross," Sam said. "And the family—all of us—have let you take it on. You shouldn't have to do it alone. Nick would want to help, too."

Tony leaned forward. "You both have careers to think about. Dad left me in charge of the hotel. Do you think I can't handle it?"

"This is not about that," Drew said sharply. "This is about someone sabotaging the place. If you think Sam and I are going to let you handle that alone, you're crazy."

"Drew—" Sam began.

"No." Drew cut off Sam with a look, then returned his gaze to Tony. "Forget your damn pride for once, Tony."

In spite of his annoyance, Tony couldn't help but admire his two younger brothers. They were double-teaming him—and they had their good-cop, bad-cop routine down pretty well. Sam, in the expensive Italian suit was the good cop, of course. And Drew, the real cop, was the bad one.

"We can do this the easy way," Drew continued, "or we can go up to the roof and Sam and I can beat it out of you."

Tony smiled then. And the smile erupted into a laugh. "You could try. But I seem to remember that the last time you made the attempt, it was not successful."

"I'd be willing to help this time," Murphy offered.

"No." All three brothers spoke in unison.

"Sooorrry!" Murphy said.

"Family only," Tony explained.

"Sam and I were kids last time," Drew pointed out. "You were a senior and you had us by fifteen pounds."

"Excuses," Tony said.

"We're tougher now," Sam said. "And meaner. And don't forget Drew here took karate classes just in case we ever talked you into a rematch."

Tony remembered it well. He'd had to walk Drew to and from the classes when his father had learned about the fight. And he'd had to take Sam to boxing lessons.

"Plus we're older. We know something about fighting dirty," Drew warned.

Tony didn't doubt it for a moment. Two against one, he had no doubt that they would beat him. Still, it would be one heck of a fight. He was almost tempted.

"But it doesn't have to come to that," Sam said. "We already know some of what's going on."

Sam had always been the intellectual one—and though he'd trained as a P.I. under their cousin Nick, he'd eventually gone to work for a high-tech security firm where they made good use of his brains.

"You had me run that check on Lily McNeil. Her father is McNeil Enterprises, and they make their money eating up small hotels. So we figure, they could be key players in this. Are we right? Are they pressuring you to sell?"

When he didn't answer right away, Tony saw temper flash into Drew's eyes.

"We're family," Drew said. "And this is our home. We have a right to know."

They were right. Tony couldn't think of one good argument against the case they'd made. "McNeil Enterprises made me an offer a month ago. Two weeks later, I received a higher offer from Fortescue Investments."

"And you didn't think that was important enough to tell us?" Drew asked, the temper flashing in his eyes again.

"There wasn't anything to tell," Tony said. "I refused both offers."

"Lucy says that Lily McNeil from McNeil Enterprises checked into the penthouse suite last night," Sam said. "According to Lucy, she's here to advise you on renovations."

"On the same night that someone sabotages our plumbing," Drew pointed out.

Tony met Drew's eyes steadily. "Lily McNeil would not be involved in sabotage."

"And you know that because?" Drew asked.

"I know that she wouldn't do something like that," Tony said.

Always the peacemaker, Sam raised both hands, palms out. "Okay. We're willing to take your word on that. But that doesn't mean that McNeil isn't behind the sabotage."

"Don't shut us out," Drew said. "We can help."

Tony sighed. "Okay. Maybe you can. Dad once told me that under no circumstances was I ever supposed to sell to McNeil. I sensed that there was some bad blood there. Does either of you know anything about it?"

Drew frowned. "The name doesn't ring a bell."

Sam smiled slowly and rubbed his hands together. "I'll check into it. If there's a connection, I bet I can dig it up. And I'll check on Fortescue, too."

"I've got a twenty that says I can dig up something before you can," Drew said.

"You're on," Sam said. Then both brothers turned to look at Tony.

He shook his head. The battle was a long and ongoing one. Sam used technology, and Drew believed in old-fashioned footwork. And though one worked for a private firm and the other for the NYPD, there weren't two better investigators in the city. "Count me out. That way I can root for both of you."

Over Drew's shoulder, Tony saw Lily step out of the elevator. For a moment, everything else slipped from his mind. She was dressed in a neat, very businesslike suit, navy pinstripes with a crisp white blouse. He could picture exactly what she was wearing underneath—the merest wisps of silk and lace. For a moment, he could have sworn that he caught her scent—lilies, the kind his mother used to grow in pots on the roof. Tony didn't notice that his brothers had followed the direction of his gaze.

Sam's voice was a distant echo when he said, "Uh-oh. We've got big trouble."

LILY HAD TAKEN GREAT CARE to dress for success. She had regrouped in the shower, recaptured her focus. Never mind that Ben Franklin's words had formed a little background chorus in her head—*early to bed, early to rise*... Oh, she'd gone *early to bed* with Tony Romano all right. She hadn't even introduced herself first! But she was not about to let it become the disaster Dame Vera had predicted. She would start all over with Tony Romano. Clean slate. She would meet him on a strictly business level, and she would do the job her father was depending on her to do.

Usually the clothes helped her. She'd chosen the pinstriped suit because of its General Patton, don't-give-me-any-crap quality. One of many tips for fighting your way to success that she'd picked up at her recent seminar was Jack Nicholson's often quoted advice to other actors: "Let the costume do the work." From now on she was determined to do just that.

However, her suit stopped working the moment she stepped out of the elevator and saw that Tony's eyes were on her. The kick-ass outfit offered no defense against the wave of heat that rolled right through her. Was she ever going to be able to see the man without remembering what they'd done to each other in that bed?

Was she ever going to see him without wanting to do it again?

The thought had her stopping short, and for one long moment she was torn between wanting to run toward him—or as far away as she could get.

So much for her clean-slate plan. Maybe what she needed was a better costume—something from the Metropolitan Museum's medieval armor collection, perhaps. On second thought, she wouldn't need it—not if she remained paralyzed forever right here in the middle of the lobby. And it wasn't only Tony who was looking at her. The other three men at his table were also staring in her direction. Two of them had to be Romanos. They'd been in the photo with Tony.

"Lily, there you are."

The sound of Lucy's voice broke her trance, and Lily

turned just as the girl took her arm. "Are you ready for your tour?"

"Yes," Lily managed to say, grateful to find she could move again when Lucy urged her toward a small gift shop that opened off the lobby.

"Grace is going to take you because I'm covering for her on registration. She has to study. Law school."

It wasn't a gift shop, exactly, Lily discovered as Lucy drew her into the small, distinctly feminine store. She took in the mannequins and the shelves displaying a variety of women's clothing—from simple T-shirts and shells to suits and cocktail dresses. And she recognized the label at once. *Gina R.*

For the second time since she'd stepped off the elevator, Lily stopped dead in her tracks. "You carry clothes by *Gina R* in your hotel gift shop?"

Lucy laughed as she urged her forward. "That's all we carry. C'mon. I'll introduce you. Mom will love that you recognize her designs."

There were two women behind the small counter at the back of the shop. One, Lily judged to be in her late forties or early fifties. She wore her dark hair pulled back and tied with a scarf. The other was younger— with the same dark hair pulled back—no scarf. She was studying Lily through the narrow glasses perched on her nose. The older woman smiled at her. The younger one didn't.

"Lily McNeil, meet my Mom, Gina Romano, and my sister, Grace," Lucy said.

Lily found her hand enveloped in the older woman's. "I'm wearing one of your suits."

"I recognize it, and I'm thrilled," Gina said.

"Lily's a consultant, and she's going to talk Tony

into turning Uncle Henry's penthouse into a restaurant," Lucy explained.

Lily felt a pang of guilt as she withdrew her hand from Gina's warm clasp. She should never have led Lucy to believe that. Her goal was to find the weaknesses of the hotel so that her father could exploit them. She wasn't supposed to be giving the Romanos false hopes. In an attempt to change the subject, she glanced around the small shop again, then said to Gina, "I had no idea that you ran your own shop."

"I won't for much longer," Gina said. "Now that my clothes are being carried in Bloomingdale's and upscale boutiques across the country, I'm finding that I don't get much business here anymore."

"You should," Lily said. "If I had known you were here, I would have made the trip."

"Maybe once," Gina said. "And then you'd find a more convenient location. This area is a little off the beaten path for shopping."

Lily moved toward the door of the shop and studied the lobby for a moment. "It wouldn't take much to make this place a destination. All we'd have to do is renovate the lobby, add some potted plants, a string quartet, and serve a really outstanding high tea. Look how many people visit the Plaza just to have a drink at the Palm Court or the Oak Room. I'm sure with the right menu, the right publicity, you wouldn't have any trouble getting women to come here for an afternoon of shopping and lunch or tea."

"Isn't she wonderful?" Lucy asked. "I told you."

Lily didn't miss that Lucy's last remark was directed to Grace. Not that Grace looked one bit convinced by Lucy's endorsement. Smart girl, Lily thought. Because the suggestions she was making were not going to be implemented by Tony Romano. She wasn't sure they would ever be implemented. Once McNeil Enterprises took over the hotel, her father had made it clear that he had a team ready to bring the hotel up to McNeil standards. Lily had not been offered a place on that team.

"If you can convince Tony to go along with that, my hat's off to you," Gina said. "He's like the rock of Gibraltar, and he likes to keep things the same. It took me two years to convince him to let me phase out the touristy stuff the gift shop used to carry."

"Tony is in a rut," Lucy said.

"He can't help it," Lily found herself saying. "An old hotel like this can be a bit of work. It just needs a face-lift."

"I can relate to that," Gina said with a laugh.

"He won't listen to anything I suggest," Lucy said.

"He's doing the best he can." And he was going to fail. Lily didn't say it out loud, but there was a little twist of pain around her heart as she thought it. Unless there was an influx of money into Henry's Place, sooner or later, Tony Romano was going to have to sell the hotel. McNeil could do wonders with the place, and the hotel deserved to be cared for and preserved. She had to focus on that.

"And you're here to help him out?" Grace asked. Her tone suggested that she didn't believe that, not for a moment, and it earned a questioning look from both Lucy and Gina.

In the time it took her to meet Grace's eyes, the pain around Lily's heart twisted tighter. "I'm here to consult with Tony on improvements he could make."

For a moment, Grace didn't speak. Then she said, "I guess that's my cue to show you around."

Lily turned to smile at Gina. "As long as we end the tour back here so that I can shop."

"Not a problem," Gina said. "I've trained my girls well. All roads lead to *Gina R.*"

In spite of the fact that Tony was still seated at the table with the three other men, Lily managed to follow Grace through the lobby without slipping into paralysis again. She felt his glance as if it were a physical touch on her skin, but she didn't falter. The moment the elevator doors slid shut, she turned to Grace. "You have a problem with me, don't you?"

Grace peered at her through the glasses. "Yes. Lucy has been singing your praises since she woke me up this morning. She thinks you're some sort of fairy godmother who's going to make all her dreams come true. She and Tony are the optimists in the family. Ever since I started law school, they've called me the cynic, and I did a little checking on you. You're from McNeil Enterprises, and they make a habit of gobbling up little hotels like Henry's Place for snacks. I don't believe that you're here to help Tony out, and I'm going to tell him so."

Lily lifted her chin. "He knows who I am. None of you seem to give him enough credit. Do you think he would have agreed to see me without running the same kind of background check that you did?"

Grace studied her for a minute. "Okay, I'll buy that. But I also know that the two of you shared the penthouse suite last night. I was studying late, and I sometimes go up to the roof to clear my head before I can go to sleep. Lucy had told me you were there, and I saw Tony go in. He didn't come out.''

Lily felt her temper rise. ''So you think I'm some kind of corporate shark who is sleeping with your cousin so that McNeil Enterprises can come along and gobble up the hotel?''

''I'm concerned about that. Yes.''

''Don't you have any faith in Tony at all? Do you think that any woman could make a fool of him that way?''

The elevator slid to a stop and the doors opened, but Grace didn't move for a moment. She merely studied Lily. ''That's the third time since I've met you that you've rushed to his defense.''

''He needs someone to defend him,'' Lily said. ''You all seem to take him for granted. You have no idea what kind of a job it is to keep a small hotel like this running and serving its guests.''

Grace's lips twitched. ''I think I do. I have to help him do it—most of the time. I used to think of it as child labor when I was younger. Now I think it's just slavery.''

Lily followed Grace onto the roof of the hotel. The penthouse that she'd spent the night in was at the far corner surrounded by tall plants. The section of the roof they were on now held a garden, all of it in pots. Beyond them were picnic tables, an outdoor grill, and a full-size basketball court.

''Do you play?'' Grace asked.

Lily shook her head. ''I'm not good at sports.''

''They won't take that as an excuse on Sunday afternoon. Sam's wife, A.J., is pregnant and she's our star player. We'll need someone to fill in for her.''

"Not me," Lily said.

"If you're still here, you'll play," Grace warned. "Tony can be very persuasive."

Lily felt the heat rise in her cheeks as she recalled just how persuasive Tony could be. She also felt that she'd passed some sort of little test with Grace. The Romano family was beginning to accept her. That's what she wanted, wasn't it? She pressed a fist against her heart where the little band of pain was getting tighter.

"I thought we'd start our tour at the top and work our way down," Grace said.

"Sounds good." By the time they reached the lobby again, Lily would have a whole list of weaknesses that she could report to her father. At the top of the list was the fact that the roof space was being wasted.

There was no black cloud over her head today. No siree. She was making great, uninterrupted progress toward the goal of gobbling up Henry's Place. Which was just what she wanted.

"ARE YOU SURE YOU KNOW what you're doing?" Sam spoke the question out loud, but it was in the eyes of both his brothers.

"I have a plan," Tony said. Murphy had left to check on the crew he had working on the eighth floor, and Sam and Drew had been grilling him ever since.

"Then it's high time you shared it," Drew said, then shifted impatiently in his chair. "If you don't talk to us about this, how can we help?"

"If it's money you need, I can talk to A.J.," Sam offered. Sam's wife had inherited money when her parents died, and Tony didn't doubt for a minute that she'd come up with whatever sum Sam asked her for.

"No," he said.

"If you don't want to go to her, Nick would come up with anything you'd ask," Drew pointed out.

"I'm not taking anyone's money if all I can do is throw it into a black hole. This place needs more than repairs if it's going to start turning a real profit. It needs a major renovation."

Sam stared at Tony. "Well, that's the most you've ever shared with us about the running of this place."

"Henry's Place is in that much trouble?" Drew asked.

"Yeah. It's in that much trouble. And Dad made me promise to keep it running," Tony said.

"You know, it's not like we really need it as a family home anymore. Gina is making enough money now that she could easily take Lucy and Grace and move into an apartment uptown," Sam said. "I have an apartment, and Drew could find one. It would be all right by all of us if you had to sell."

"I promised Dad I wouldn't." Tony smiled. "Besides, I told you I have a plan."

"And sleeping with the enemy is part of it?" Drew asked with a sudden frown.

Tony shot him a look. "I'm assuming you're using that phrase figuratively."

"Sam and I saw the way you looked at her when she stepped out of the elevator," Drew said.

He was not going to discuss Lily with them. But his brothers knew him very well—as well as he knew them. And they'd always been able to tell if one or the other of them was interested in a woman.

"Lily's here as a consultant. She's going to make suggestions and draw up a financial plan so that I can make improvements on the hotel that will put us well into the black again," Tony said. "And she's very good at what she does. Sam checked her out."

"Her former employer—a small exclusive European chain—valued her creativity. But that doesn't mean she's here to share it with you. How much is she charging for this consultation?"

"Nothing," Tony said.

"There's a red flag," Drew said. "If it sounds too good to be true, it usually is."

"She could be here spying for her father's company. And Grace is giving her the grand tour," Sam said, shaking his head. "I don't like it."

"I'll deal with her," Tony said, and tried to deflect his brothers' attention. "But what I don't need is anymore sabotage. Can either of you do something about that?"

"I know a couple of freelance P.I.s who owe me a favor. They can take turns on surveillance," Sam said. "I'm also going to dig a little more into McNeil Enterprises and see if I can find any history of *problems* before they come in and do one of their buy-outs."

"Good idea," Drew said. "I'll keep an eye out when I'm around here. And I'll put out the word and see if some of my informants know who might have cut the pipes. Murphy said they knew what they were doing."

As Sam and Drew continued to plot a defense against future sabotage attempts, Tony glanced around the lobby. Lucy was busy at the registration desk with two businessmen who were snappy dressers. Alistair had joined Dame Vera, and she'd taken out her crystal. Outside the glass entrance doors, he saw that a steady rain had started to fall and he glanced at his watch. Hopefully, it would lighten up before he and Lily took their run. Either way, when they came back from it, they'd have to shower. Just thinking about the possibilities had his lips curving.

"You want to share the joke?" Drew asked.

Tony clamped down on the image that had begun to fill his mind and shifted his gaze to his brother. "I'm going to have a word with Dame Vera and Alistair. I don't know anyone who spends more time checking the comings and goings of everyone, and I think they'd enjoy becoming amateur sleuths, don't you?"

Tony had started to rise from his chair when he heard Grace's laughter, then saw his sister and Lily step out of the elevator. "Well, it looks like Lily and Grace have hit it off."

Sam frowned. "Grace isn't won over easily. All the more reason for you to watch your back, bro."

A difficult maneuver, Tony thought. How was he supposed to watch his back when he couldn't seem to take his eyes off Lily McNeil? The tour had taken nearly forty minutes, and he'd found himself glancing at his watch no less than three times.

He'd missed seeing her. He'd missed being in the same room with her. He'd missed *her*. The stream of realizations rocked him.

Desire was one thing. He was quite comfortable with the fact that he wanted her in bed again—soon. He was even enjoying the latest little fantasy playing around the edges of his mind on just how he was going to get her out of that very businesslike suit. The scenario centered on the lacy little bow on the blouse she was wearing. He imagined untying it, and then slowly unbuttoning her blouse while he watched nothing but her eyes.

He was going to turn that fantasy into reality, but he wanted more than that from Lily McNeil. He wanted to get to know her. He wanted some part of that easy camaraderie that his cousin Grace had seemed to find with her.

Sam was right. He damned well better watch his back.

WHEN GRACE HUGGED HER, Lily felt like a complete slug again. The fact that she could feel Tony watching her made her feel worse than a slug. Lightning chose that moment to flash outside the glass entrance doors, and her stomach plummeted even further.

"I have to go," Grace said. "I have a big constitutional law test on Monday, but I'll see you at the basketball game on Sunday. Tony will drag you there."

She was doing her job, Lily tried to tell herself as Grace's arms tightened briefly around her before letting her go. And her job was to make sure Tony Romano sold out to McNeil Enterprises. That was what she wanted, Lily reminded herself. As she watched Grace step back into the elevator, she again felt like a traitor.

Getting what she wanted was now within her reach. She knew exactly what the weaknesses in the hotel were—plumbing, a restaurant that was seldom filled to capacity, poorly utilized space, and rooms that were in dire need of renovation. Her father would make good use of the information. But her notebook was also filled with ideas for turning Henry's Place into a profitable small luxury hotel. She hadn't been able to prevent herself from jotting down her ideas. Of course, she would present them to Tony in her "fake" consulting report along with a financial plan. She'd jotted down some notes on the latter, also.

Lily sighed. There was a part of her that wanted to implement the ideas she'd come up with. This was just the kind of work she'd excelled at when she'd worked for the Marchmount Hotel chain in Europe. Unfortunately, her skills wouldn't be put to use at McNeil.

Lightning flashed again, and this time thunder growled. Lily whirled toward the entrance doors to the hotel and saw that a pouring rain had started to fall. Out of the corner of her eye, she saw Dame Vera on her settee. As she shifted her gaze to meet the older woman's, Dame Vera's earlier words echoed in her mind as clearly as if the woman had spoken them out loud again. *Beware the Ides of March. Disaster is near.*

"Lily? What are you doing here?"

Lily recognized the voice even before she turned. Still, she wasn't prepared for the sight of the two men walking toward her from the hotel entrance. Her stepbrother, a mix of disapproval and annoyance on his face, was bad enough. Her father had given her his word—the Romano job was hers. Had he changed his mind? Didn't he trust her at all?

But even as the questions streamed through her mind, she couldn't prevent her attention from shifting to the second man—Giles Fortescue, her ex-fiancé and ex-lover. It was the first time since she'd broken off her engagement that she'd seen him. Not one disaster, but two were striding toward her. A double whammy, and she felt it in her stomach like a blow.

Her notebook was the first thing to slip away from

her. It hit the floor with a splat. Even worse, she could feel all of her newfound confidence begin seeping away as surely as if she'd been pricked by a hundred little pins. Her one thought was that she had to plug the leaks.

The next thing she knew, Giles captured one of her hands and raised it to his lips.

"I can't believe my eyes," he said. "I thought for sure that Jerry was mistaken when he called your name. You've changed."

Thunder growled more fiercely, and Lily struggled to gather her thoughts and her confidence. She wasn't the naive girl Giles had so easily seduced, and she would not be taken in by him again. She *had* changed. She was the new Lily. She could gobble up hotels with the best of them.

"I'll take that as a compliment, Giles." She managed a smile. "What brings you to Henry's Place?"

"You," he said. "I learned through the grapevine that you were scheduled to come here on behalf of McNeil Enterprises, and I decided to take a little vacation and join you."

He was so smooth, Lily thought, from the words right down to the gentle way he was massaging her hand. Two years ago the charm and the intensity of his gaze as he looked at her would have worked. But she was discovering that the new Lily didn't believe a word he was saying. Whatever the reason he'd come to Henry's Place it wasn't to join her. She was willing to put money on it and on the fact that his presence was a clear indication that McNeil Enterprises wasn't the only company interested in buying out Tony Romano. Though she was curious about that, she had bigger fish to fry. Turning to her brother, she said, "What brings you here, Jerry?"

"You're supposed to be stuck in Tahiti." Leaning over, Jerry picked up the notebook that she'd dropped. "J.R. sent me to meet with Romano in your place."

"That won't be necessary since I'm here, and I've already met once with him."

Instead of handing her the notebook, Jerry began to leaf through the pages. "Looks like you've been busy." The smile he sent her when he glanced up was cool and superior. "Since I'm here, I'll be happy to take your preliminary ideas back to J.R."

Lily wanted to kick him. Instead, she extracted her hand from Giles's grip and extended it, palm out. "That notebook is mine, and when I'm ready to present my ideas, I'll deliver them in person."

Jerry held the notebook just out of her reach.

"Since you haven't bothered to call in, I'm under orders to report back to J.R," he said. "I'll just pass this along."

"The lady wants her notebook back," Tony said.

Lily nearly jumped. She'd been so focused on the two men in front of her that she hadn't heard Tony approach. Out of the corner of her eye, she saw that he'd brought the two men who'd been sitting with him.

"This is a family matter," Jerry said. "The lady is my stepsister."

"What a coincidence," Tony said with a smile. "My brothers and I are making this a family matter, too. The lady is a guest of our hotel, and we're asking you nicely to give her back her notebook."

Or else.

Not one of the Romano men spoke the words, but

Lily heard them clearly in the silence. Jerry's color was rising, but he wasn't extending the notebook. For the first time, she noted that Giles had distanced himself from the confrontation, slipping back toward the registration desk.

Jerry stood his ground. She couldn't help but admire him a bit for that. For the space of five long seconds, the four men said nothing, but Lily could hear the tension ratcheting up between them as clearly as if someone were cranking it. Testosterone seemed to crackle in the air.

Taking a deep breath, she reached out, closed her fingers around the notebook and tugged it free of Jerry's grip. "Thank you," she said and smiled sweetly at her stepbrother. "I don't think Father would appreciate it if you got into a fight with any member of the Romano family."

The whole scene was almost worth the quick flush of humiliation that flashed across Jerry's face. She'd pay for it, of course. But it would be worth the price.

With a brief nod to the three men behind her, Jerry stalked off and exited through the revolving doors.

That was the good news, Lily decided. At least Jerry hadn't registered to stay in the hotel and spy on her. The bad news was that Giles had. She caught a brief glimpse of him taking a key from Lucy before she turned to Tony. "Thank you."

"Not a problem."

It occurred to her then that no one in her family had ever taken her side or come to her defense the way the Romanos just had, and for a brief moment, she'd felt an odd sense of belonging.

A bit flustered by the sensation, she turned to the other two men. "And thank you, too."

"Sam and Drew, I'd like you to meet Lily McNeil."

Sam and Drew nodded at her in turn, but their eyes were almost as cool as her stepbrother's had been. Neither extended a hand. That was fair. She told herself it was relief she was feeling and not disappointment.

"They have to get to work," Tony said.

For a second neither of them moved. Then Sam turned to Tony. "I'll call you as soon as I get something."

"Ditto," said Drew as he turned with Sam and headed toward the revolving doors.

"I thought they'd never leave," Tony said in a low tone.

She couldn't prevent her lips from curving as she turned to him. He was looking at her and not his brothers, and the quiet intensity of his gaze made the breath stop in her throat. On some level, she was aware that people streamed around them, moving into and out of the lobby, but for a second, she had the strangest sensation that time had slowed, narrowing to this moment and this man.

"Who's the man who kissed your hand?" he asked.

The question helped her regain her focus and she shifted her gaze to Giles who was moving toward the elevator. "My ex-fiancé, Giles Fortescue."

Tony's gaze narrowed. "From Fortescue Investments?"

She nodded.

"Do you still care for him?"

The question was so unexpected that Lily answered

before she thought. "No." Then, finding that it was true, she turned to Tony again. "No."

"Good."

Before she could sense his intention, he gripped her shoulders, urging her upward ever so slightly so that she rose on her tiptoes. Then his mouth covered hers.

The kiss was everything she remembered—possessive, demanding. And at the same time, his mouth was so soft and fit so perfectly against hers. Pleasure streamed through her. She should push him away. But she couldn't seem to feel her arms. She couldn't feel anything but the warm sense of belonging that had moved through her before. Enticing. Irresistible.

Then his teeth scraped against her bottom lip and a new round of sensations erupted. Pleasure turned sharp—pinprick explosions of it raced along every nerve ending. Why would she ever consider pushing him away? How could she when he made her feel this way? The heat came next. His hands gripped her shoulders, his mouth moved on hers. They touched nowhere else, and yet she could have sworn that flames licked along her skin and flared deep in her center. Nothing, no one had ever made her feel this...wanted. And she wanted the feeling to last....

As suddenly as he'd begun, Tony broke off the kiss. His hands dropped to his side and Lily found herself standing on legs she couldn't feel.

"We'd better take this somewhere more private," Tony murmured.

Later, she would wonder what she might have said if she hadn't just that moment caught sight of Jerry staring at her through the glass entrance doors. A short distance away, Tony's brothers stood on the curb, and they were watching the scene, too.

"No."

"No?"

"No." It was even harder to say the second time. She didn't think her mind had ever been more at odds with her body. But she was the new Lily. And she was supposed to know what she wanted. "I'm not going anywhere private with you."

She wasn't going to look at him. If she did, she was almost sure her resolve would collapse. But she could feel him shift his gaze to the entrance doors of the hotel just in time to see Jerry step into a taxi.

"You're a tough nut to crack, Lily McNeil."

Not true, she thought. Tony Romano had gotten through her shell, and he'd just made sure that pretty much everyone knew it.

"Good thing I'm a patient man," he said as he urged her toward the elevator.

What she needed was some time to thicken her shell again. Some time to regroup and clean that slate off. And she needed to do it alone. As he nudged her onto the elevator, she said, "I need some time to think."

"It won't help."

She looked at him then.

He shrugged. "I've already given it my best shot, and for the life of me, I can't figure out what I'm going to do about what's happening between us."

Her eyes narrowed. "Well, I'll give it *my* best shot and I'll let you know."

He grinned and ran a finger down her nose. "You have a habit of squinting your eyes just before you fire off both barrels. It's cute."

She had her mouth open ready to fire them off again when the elevator doors slid open.

"Half an hour," Tony said as he nudged her through the doors, then stepped back. "That's when we're scheduled for our run."

As the doors of the elevator slid shut, separating them, Lily tried to focus on the bright side. The good news was that Tony was not coming up with her to the penthouse suite. The bad news was that she wanted him to.

5

SLIPPING INTO THE ELEVATOR with Lily was something that Tony debated doing right up until the second that the doors slid all the way shut. He might have done it if he hadn't needed to take care of some business before he joined Lily for her run. He'd spoken nothing less than the truth when he'd told his brothers that Lily wasn't involved in any kind of sabotage, but he wasn't at all sure that he could put something like that past her father or her stepbrother. Or someone else?

There was something hovering around the edges of his memory—something that had been nearly dredged up when Dame Vera had mentioned the Ides of March. He was almost certain that was the day that Lily had first called to talk him into seeing her. That's when he would have heard her voice for the first time. The day planner he kept in his office would help him remember. But first, he needed to talk to Dame Vera and Alistair.

When he turned and headed toward them, he noted that the teapot had disappeared, and Dame Vera was now gazing intently into her crystal. He moved quickly toward them and seated himself across from her. Whatever she was staring at in the crystal had all of her attention, and for a moment, he hesitated.

"You're thinking about the Ides of March," she said as she raised her gaze to meet his. "Good."

"Sometimes, I really wonder about you, Dame Vera," Tony said.

Behind his paper, Alistair chuckled. "Join the club."

"That will be quite enough, Alistair," Dame Vera said. "I'd send you away, but Anthony has come to ask us both a favor."

"How did you—" Tony cut himself off and said, "Never mind. I do need your help."

Alistair lowered his paper and drew his chair closer. "Something rotten in Denmark, old boy?"

Tony debated for a moment about how much he should tell them. These two were part of the responsibility that his father had turned over to him with the hotel, and he didn't want to worry them unnecessarily.

Dame Vera closed her eyes for a moment. "Something about the plumbing."

"You might as well spill it," Alistair said. "She'll eventually figure it out, anyway."

"The plumbing problem wasn't just a catastrophe of aging pipes," Tony said, keeping his voice low. "Murphy says someone deliberately and very cleverly cut the pipes."

"Disaster is near," Dame Vera murmured.

It might have been a trick of light—a short perhaps in the chandelier that hung from the ceiling, but Tony could have sworn he saw something move in the crystal that sat on the table.

"What can we do to help?" Alistair asked.

"First, I want to know if you've noticed anyone in the hotel—someone dressed as a delivery person or a repair person of any kind. Someone you've never seen before."

Dame Vera and Alistair looked at one another, then

turned to Tony and spoke in unison. "The exterminator."

"He came to my door early yesterday morning, and said that he was doing my suite and all the rooms underneath," Dame Vera said. "I was still in my nighttime attire. I hadn't even had my tea. He told me I had to leave and not return for two hours, so that the insecticide would have time to fade away."

Alistair took one of her hands and raised it to his lips. "And we spent a very enjoyable morning together, my dear."

Vera extracted her hand and turned to Tony. "I accused Alistair of hiring him on purpose as a ploy to get me into his apartment."

Alistair raised both hands. "I pleaded innocent, but she didn't believe me."

"Can you describe him?" Tony asked.

"I can do better than that." Alistair pulled a pen from his smoking jacket and drew a napkin closer.

"He's not a bad sketch artist," Vera explained. "If he hadn't made it in acting, he could have been a painter."

Alistair paused for a moment and winked at Tony. "She should know. She's seen my etchings often enough."

Because he thought it was prudent, Tony bit back a grin. But he had to agree with Dame Vera's assessment as a face began to take shape on the napkin. "That's the man," Dame Vera announced when Alistair finally lifted his pen.

"Thanks," Tony said. "I'm going to fax this to Drew, and see if he can come up with a match in one of the mug books down at the precinct."

"Good idea," Vera said. "What else can we do?"

"I want the two of you to keep your eyes and ears open. If you see anyone like this exterminator—or anyone else—even a guest—who seems to be acting suspicious, let me know."

Dame Vera's eyes lit up. "Excellent. It's always been a secret dream of mine to be cast in one of the *Thin Man* movies. Myrna Loy and William Powell always looked like they were having so much fun playing Nick and Nora Charles."

"It probably had something to do with the vast number of martinis they were always drinking," Alistair said.

"Sam is sending over a couple of men to keep an eye out. I'll introduce them to you." Tony rose and then remembered. "About the Ides of March, Dame Vera, can you tell me anything more specific?"

Vera shook her head. "Lily is the one to ask about that."

LILY STARED AT HER IMAGE in the bathroom mirror. The woman staring back at her was the new Lily—slender and fit in running shorts and a T-shirt that fit like a second skin. This Lily could have whatever she wanted.

She had to believe in that. The problem was she had to make sure she remembered what that was. And it wasn't—it couldn't—be Tony Romano. She stole a quick glance at her watch and prayed she could remember that when she saw him ten minutes from now.

Ten minutes. That was all she had to regroup. After hurrying into the bedroom, she picked up the pen and message pad that lay on the bedside table. Her island guru had preached writing down your goals. People who did were about ninety percent more certain of achieving them.

She printed the words. "I want Henry's Place." Then tearing off the page, she climbed up on the bed and placed it in front of her. Once she was in the lotus position, she stared down at the paper, then closed her eyes and pictured the words in her mind. Visualization was also a powerful tool, and she needed all the help she could get. After drawing in a deep breath, she let it out on the count of ten while she formed an image in her mind. She was walking into her father's office, carrying her report on Henry's Place. She could see her father open it, and then he smiled at her. "Good job."

Those were two words he'd never spoken to her, not even when she'd graduated first in her class at Stanford. And she was so close to hearing him say them. All she had to do was—

The chiming bells of her cell phone had the image fading from her mind. She pulled the phone from her purse and glanced at the caller ID, then felt a quick skip of panic. Her father. Jerry had wasted no time letting J. R. McNeil know what he'd seen through the glass doors of the lobby. One of these days, she was really going to have to kick her stepbrother. Hard. Drawing in a deep breath, she said, "Hello, Dad."

"What in hell do you think you're doing?"

"I'm doing what you asked me to do," she said. "I'm getting information on Henry's Place for you."

There was a beat of silence on the other end of the phone. "Are you sleeping with Romano?"

J. R. McNeil was not known for beating around the bush. But Lily hadn't been his daughter for twenty-five years for nothing. This time she was one jump ahead of him. She'd already crossed her fingers. "No."

Of course, technically, she was telling the truth. She was not sleeping with Tony Romano right now. Although they had made love—several times—on the very bed she was sitting on.

Outside the window, lightning flashed and lit up the darkening sky.

Wincing a little, Lily began to pleat the edge of the bedspread between her fingers as she listened to a short silence on the other end of the line.

Then another voice, much fainter, said, "You never should have sent her. She's going to ruin this for us, and we have to have that hotel."

Lily recognized the speaker—Pamela Langford-McNeil.

"You have to replace her with Jerry before—"

The sound was abruptly cut off. Lily knew exactly what her father was doing—pacing back and forth behind his desk and frowning. She'd seen him do the same thing the day he'd finally agreed to let her take on the job of making sure that Tony Romano sold Henry's Place to McNeil Enterprises. He always paced when he had to make a decision.

Pamela would be in front of his desk, her voice controlled but determined, cataloguing all of Lily's past failures. It was a scene she'd witnessed many times before, and her usual reaction had been to run away and try to fight another battle on another day.

"I don't think you can handle this on your own," her father finally said.

"Yes, I can," she replied as the pain in her chest sharpened. Would he ever just simply believe in her?

"Kissing Romano in the lobby. What were you thinking? You're not falling for him, are you?"

"No." Just the thought brought on another skip of panic. She couldn't be falling for him. She'd only just met him. And slept with him. And she wanted to sleep with again. But that wasn't love.

"Dammit, Lily, I'm sending Jerry in to help you," he said finally. "This deal is crucial. When I heard you were stuck in Tahiti, I thought it was for the best. We aren't the only ones who want that hotel, and Jerry has more experience. I've brought him up to speed. He's all set to handle this."

Lily tightened her grip on the phone. She was not going to give way. "We had an agreement. This is my job. Jerry nearly got into a fight with Tony and his two brothers. Did he tell you that?"

There was another stretch of silence.

"I've already established a friendly rapport with the Romanos." At least with some of them. "Your best bet right now is me." She had all of her fingers crossed as she held her breath.

There was another beat of silence. "This is a crucial deal."

"Dad, I can handle it." Closing her eyes, she tried to ignore the headache that was beginning to pound behind her eyes. One thing she was discovering about the new Lily—she was learning to lie like a pro. "I'll get you what you want."

Lily counted three beats this time and held her breath.

"I'm depending on you."

Before she could reply, her father cut the connection, but she held on to the open phone, just staring down at it. Her father had always been a man of few words. Hello, goodbye, how are you, and I love you—those words were simply not part of his vocabulary.

She sighed as she dropped her head in her hands. The good news was he hadn't fired her or sent Jerry. The bad news was he was depending on her to deliver Henry's Place. Neither made her want to celebrate.

You can have anything you want.

The words had barely formed themselves in her mind when she sensed that Tony was there in the room with her. How long had he been there? How much had he heard? Ignoring the panic bubbling away in her stomach, she tried to rerun her conversation. What had she said? "I'm getting information on Henry's Place for you." Not good. "I'll get you what you want." Even worse. As a spy, she would never make the 007 level. James Bond would probably never even choose her as one of his girls. And she couldn't sit here with her head buried in her hands forever.

"Lily?"

Glancing up, she met Tony's eyes, and for a moment the pleasure of seeing him wiped every thought and concern from her mind.

A black T-shirt fit him like a second skin. Worn gray sweats hugged his hips and only emphasized the length of those lean, muscled legs. The man gave new meaning to the word *gorgeous*. All she had to do was look at him and she wanted him. It was that simple, that terrifying.

As her skin heated along with her thoughts, she remembered that she was sitting on the bed they'd made love on only hours earlier. Was he thinking about that too? Was he feeling even part of what she was feeling?

Even as the questions raced through her mind, Tony moved to the foot of the bed. "What exactly did your father say to you?"

The words triggered one skip of panic, then a second. The third was far more than a skip. It was a full-blown wave. Was her cover completely blown?

"Nothing." She dropped her gaze from his as she tucked her cell phone into her purse and edged herself off the side of the bed.

"He said something." Tony had a pretty good idea what the conversation had been about. Any doubt that she was part of her father's plot to get his hands on Henry's Place had vanished as he'd stood in the doorway and listened to her side of the conversation. He'd deal with that later. Right now he was going to deal with the expression on her face when her father had ended the call. It took him only two steps to circle the bed and reach her. "Whatever he said to you, it made you sad."

"He's concerned that I'm not doing my job. That's nothing new."

He tilted her chin up so that she had to meet his eyes. The mix of fear and sadness had a knot tightening in his stomach. He thought he understood the fear. She was wondering just how long he'd been standing there eavesdropping on her conversation. She definitely had secrets to hide. But he couldn't ignore the sadness. It pulled at him, angered him. She'd looked so forlorn, almost defeated, when she'd finished talking to her father. He'd wanted nothing more than to go to her and take her in his arms.

But he wouldn't have stopped with merely holding her. He would have done what he'd been thinking about doing all morning. What he wanted to do right now. He would have made love to her. And he wasn't at all sure that's what she needed.

In the time he'd taken to change his clothes, he'd promised himself that he was going to give her time. He was going to give them both some time.

But he needed to do something about the sadness.

"Why would your father doubt that you would do your job?" he asked. His own father had never once doubted that he could take over the responsibility of running the hotel. He wondered for a moment just how different his life would have been if his dad hadn't had that kind of faith in him.

"It's a long story," she said.

"We've got some time." Tony nodded his head toward the window. "That rain is still in the downpour stage." When she still hesitated, he said, "At least give me the *Reader's Digest* version."

She sighed. "In a nutshell, he's never believed that I could be successful in an executive position at McNeil Enterprises. He let me know that for the first time when I was ten, and ever since then I've been determined to prove him wrong. So far, it's been a standoff. The fact that my stepbrother just called him to report that I was kissing you in the lobby has brought back all of his doubts about my competence. And my stepmother is right there, chanting my past failures at him like a Greek chorus."

"A Greek chorus, huh?" Tony smiled at her. "I've got my share of them around here, too. Let me tell you how I see it. First off, your stepbrother is a jerk."

Lily's lips curved and some of her tension eased. "We can agree about that, at least."

"You're beautiful when you smile. Did you know that?" He traced a finger along her cheek where a flush at his words tinted her skin.

"I'm not beautiful," she said. "And I—"

"You're not beautiful all the time," he interrupted. "Most of the time you're merely pretty."

"Merely pretty—" Her eyes narrowed, and he was pleased to see that the last trace of sadness had vanished from her eyes—to be replaced by a hint of annoyance.

"See. There's another thing we can agree on," he pointed out.

"Thanks. I think."

He tucked a strand of hair behind her ear. "But when you smile, you take my breath away."

"I—"

The mix of pleasure and confusion that filled her eyes had him rethinking his earlier resolution to give them both some time. He wasn't sure that he could.

He slipped a finger down to where her pulse was beating frantically at her throat. "You are so responsive."

She cleared her throat and stepped back against the side of the bed. "I don't think we should talk about that."

He didn't drop his hand. "Okay. What were we talking about before—? Your brother. He reminds me a little of my brothers. I've just spent the past hour being grilled by them. They're worried that I'm going to let you lead me down the garden path, and that I'll sign over the hotel to you—or some such nonsense. Can you believe that?"

"Yes...I mean, no. I mean..."

Tony wondered if she realized how transparent her thoughts were. She was not a woman who was good at deception. Her cheeks were flushed, and she was having trouble meeting his eyes again.

"Even if you were," he continued, "they're certainly not giving me a heck of a lot of credit, thinking that I'd let you do something like that."

"Right," she managed to answer. And then she did meet his eyes. "You'd be a tough man to fool."

"Exactly. I've just spent the morning convincing them that I'm a big boy and I can take care of myself." He gripped her chin, tilting it up so that she couldn't look away. "I want to know what I can do to convince you of that, too."

"Why?"

He trailed one finger down her throat again, but he kept his eyes steady on hers. "Because I want very much to make love to you again, and I don't think you'll enjoy it until we clear some things up."

He felt the hitch in her breath and the fast beat of her pulse against his finger.

"I don't think that we should."

"Clear things up?" he asked. The running clothes she wore were slate blue and hugged every curve. He fingered the smooth, slick fabric that covered her shoulders and thought of the silky softness that lay beneath.

"I don't think we should make love again. It wouldn't be wise."

"Probably not." He lowered his head until his lips were a breath away from hers. "But it would be fun."

She turned her head to avoid his mouth. "I like to keep business and pleasure separate."

"I couldn't agree more." He traced his finger along the delicate line of her collarbone and then back to that frantically beating pulse. She raised both hands and spread them against his chest, but she wasn't pushing him away.

"Business and pleasure should always be separate," he continued, "and we're both old enough and smart enough to keep them that way, wouldn't you agree?"

"Yes, but..."

"Then it's settled. We'll talk about business when we go for that run. But right now, I think we could both use some pleasure." He drew back a little and met her eyes steadily. "I want you, Lily. I want to touch you. I want to be inside of you again when you come."

She stared at him and felt her muscles melt. How could she still be standing?

"Tell me that you don't want me, and I'll walk right out of here. All our future dealings will be strictly business."

Her throat was dry, her skin icy and hot all at once. "I can't tell you that."

He lowered his head again and closed his teeth around her bottom lip, then soothed the small pain with his tongue. "Then tell me that you want me to make love to you."

He was backing her into a corner. She thought of crossing her fingers and trying a lie, but before she could, he covered her hands and linked his fingers with hers. "Say the words, Lily."

"You don't play fair," she said.

He smiled then—a very slow smile that ruthlessly made use of his dimples. Then he leaned down and scraped his teeth against her neck, just where her pulse was pounding so furiously that she wondered how they could make themselves heard above it.

"I play to win. Tell me you want to make love with me."

She slipped her hands free and wrapped her arms around him. "I want you. I really shouldn't, but I want you so much."

"You've got me." This time the scrape of his teeth on her neck was sharper and so was the pleasure that arrowed through her. She pulled at the string on his sweatpants, but his hands gripped hers and drew them away.

"This time we are definitely going to take it slowly," he said.

"Right," she said, the challenge clear in her eyes.

She saw his lips curve at the same time that heat flashed into his eyes. He raised her hands to his lips and brushed them over one knuckle and then the other. "Very slowly, until you can think only of me. Want only me."

A shudder moved through her. Then his mouth hovered over hers. She felt his breath on her lips before he tilted his head and feathered kisses along her jaw.

"I want to see you this time. All of you. Let me undress you, Lily."

"Mmmmm." She wasn't sure she could refuse him anything.

Dropping her hands, Tony took the edge of her T-shirt and drew it up and over her head. She wore a sheer pink bra beneath, and she began to tremble as he ran one finger along the edge of it, tracing the narrow lace border and finally drifting lower to circle her nipple. Then he traced the same path on her other breast.

By the time he took his mouth on the same journey his fingers had taken, her eyes had drifted shut.

Rain hissed at the window, and time seemed to expand as Tony continued to move his hands over her. His fingers were tracing her lips, her shoulders, her arms, her ribs, as if he was determined to explore every inch of her. No one had ever made her feel this way—as if she were a fragile piece of glass.

She was still standing. Her feet had to be on the floor because she could feel the press of the bed against her hips and her legs. But she could have sworn she was floating. Her running shorts slithered down her legs. His fingers trailed up her thighs.

She heard her low moan of approval.

"I've been wanting to do this since you stepped off that elevator this morning." He ran one finger over the sheer silk of her panties until it pressed against her heat. Lily felt the slow burn turn into a flashfire.

More. She wasn't sure if she'd said the word or thought it.

He slid his finger beneath the edge of her panties. "I wanted to get you out of that neat little suit so that I could touch you like this." He slid a finger into her heat.

She erupted immediately. Her body stiffened and she called out his name as the pleasure shot through her in a huge wave that built and built and built until it crashed around her.

He was struggling against the need to hurry as he lifted her and laid her on the bed. As he peeled off his clothes and sheathed himself in a condom, he could feel his control shredding. He had to touch her again. More than the need to rush, to possess, to conquer was the need to bring her to that shuddering peak of pleasure again. He wanted that for her—for him.

He began to run his hands over her and then he used his mouth, ruthlessly exploiting the weaknesses that he'd discovered earlier. In some part of his mind, he knew that he wasn't being gentle, just as he hadn't been before. But everywhere he touched, she was waiting, willing. A man could get addicted to that kind of generosity and to the sound of her voice as she cried out his name. He had to have more. The word became a drumbeat in his head, pushing him closer and closer to the edge.

When her fingers dug into his shoulders and she arched against him, he braced over her and focused on her face. He needed to see her, her mouth swollen from his kiss, her eyes half-closed and dazed with pleasure.

He'd promised her that she'd think only of him, want only him, but as he pushed into her and felt her close around him, he thought only of Lily and wanted only her. And then he couldn't think at all. Pleasure. Ecstasy. There wasn't a word to describe what he felt as they moved together. She raced with him, matching him move for move, heartbeat for heartbeat until he felt her body stiffen. Then he drove them both over the edge.

WHEN HE FINALLY SURFACED, Tony found that he and Lily were snuggled like spoons again in the middle of the bed. Outside, the rain had stopped, and the sun was making a cameo appearance between the dark clouds that still hung over the city. The suite had become so quiet that he could hear the steady sound of Lily's breath each time she exhaled.

He didn't want to move. In fact, he was pretty certain he could have been happy lying right where he was for a very long time. A sudden thought had him stifling a laugh. Now he knew exactly what Goldilocks must have experienced when Little Bear's bed felt "just right."

Only in his case, he was pretty sure that the "just right" feeling had little to do with the bed and everything to do with the woman he was holding in his arms. Oh, she felt just right, that was for sure. He should be worried about that. But he couldn't quite work up the energy. Lily sighed in her sleep and pressed even closer to him. Tony bet that she wouldn't be quite so comfortable doing that if she was awake.

That was just one more problem he had to deal with. And then there was the sabotage. He would stand by what he'd said to his brothers. Lily had nothing to do with it. He'd checked his day planner and she had called him to make an appointment on March fifteenth. But something in his gut told him that she was not connected to any "disaster" that was headed his way. And he intended to prove it. To do that he needed more information, and his best bet for getting it was lying right in his arms.

The sudden knocking at the door had him stifling a curse. It could only be family. None of the guests in the hotel had a key to the rooftop floor. He'd slipped his arm out from under Lily, when the knock sounded again, and she stirred. A second later, she sat straight up in bed. "I'll go."

"It'll be family," Tony said. "I call dibs on murdering him or her."

"Don't be ridiculous." She slid off the side of the bed

and began to pull on her running clothes. A second later, she was out the door.

Nope. She wasn't a bit comfortable about waking up in the same bed with him. Not yet. If someone had shot a starting gun, he doubted that she could have made it out of the bedroom much faster.

His father had once confided in him that women were work. Personally, he'd never thought so himself—until now.

After sliding off the bed, he stooped down to get his sweats, and a slip of paper caught his eye. It contained one sentence in Lily's almost perfect script.

"I want Henry's Place."

Two dogs and one bone, Tony thought as he pulled on his sweats and slipped the paper in the pocket. Oh yeah, he had his work cut out for him all right. He wanted a woman who wanted to take his hotel away from him.

He definitely had his work cut out for him.

6

LILY HURRIED across the upper level of the suite and wondered what in the world she'd been thinking. But of course, she hadn't been thinking. When it came to Tony Romano, she didn't think at all. The synapses of her brain just morphed into mush. Reaching the door, she drew in a deep breath and then opened it. Then she just stared at the huge arrangement of red roses. There had to be two dozen, maybe three. There was only one person who'd ever sent her red roses—Giles Fortescue. He'd sent them to her regularly during the six months that he'd courted her. Her stomach sank as she reached for the card.

"Please join me in the cocktail lounge in the lobby of the Waldorf-Astoria at seven. For old time's sake. Giles." As quickly as if the note had singed her fingers, she tucked it back into the flowers.

"You have an admirer."

Tony moved past her to lift the vase, but she blocked the doorway when he turned. "I don't want them. Send them back."

"Too late," he said. "I don't think the florist will accept a return like this."

"No." She pressed a hand against his chest as he stepped forward. "I want them returned to Giles Fortescue. He's right here in the hotel. I saw him register."

"He can still get to you." Tony took his time setting

the flowers back down and quickly scanned the note as he did. Odd—he'd never noticed before that jealousy could pierce like an icy blade in the gut.

"No. That is..." Turning, she paced back into the suite, then whirled to face him. "I'm the one who gets to me. I'm still angry with myself that I fell for his line. I was so gullible. For six months, I thought he was in love with me." Waving a hand, she began to pace again. "Worse, I thought I was in love with him. Turns out all he wanted was a marriage that would solidify the financial arrangements between his family's company and my father's. They were planning a merger, and the wedding was part of the deal. Everyone knew all about it except me. Giles informed me two weeks before the wedding. That's when he explained to me that we would have a 'modern' marriage. Of course we would have to produce a child, but after that, we could go our separate ways." Turning toward him again, she raised a hand and tapped her forehead. "Can't you see the word *stupid* engraved right here?"

"No." Tony stepped back into the suite and closed the door on the flowers. "What's the matter with your family? Why did they treat you that way? Why didn't they tell you up front that it was a marriage of convenience?"

"'Anyone with half an ounce of common sense would have known.' That's what my stepmother said. She was astonished that I would think that someone with Giles's sophistication and taste would actually fall in love with someone like me. Or that he would even consider being faithful."

"That would be Jerry the jerk's mother?" Tony asked. He wanted to pace himself. But he would wait until the right people were around to vent his anger. "What about your father?"

"My father is all business. It probably never occurred to him that anyone would view marriage as anything but a business arrangement."

"What did you do when you found out?"

She shifted her gaze from his. "The usual. I wrote Giles a note breaking off the engagement and ran away. I'm good at running away. I'm not good at confrontations."

His eyes narrowed as he studied her for a moment. "You could have fooled me. The first time I saw you sleeping on this couch, I guessed you were a born fighter. And you were holding your own with the jerk this morning." *With me, too,* he could have added.

She met his eyes then. "The old Lily used to run away from fights. I've spent the past two years trying to turn myself into the new Lily."

"I like her," he said. And when he saw the stunned expression come into her eyes, he had to clamp down on his anger all over again. She looked as though no one had ever told her that before. What was wrong with her family? Were they too stupid to see the kind of person she was? He moved to her and gathered her into his arms. "But as much as I like the new Lily, I think I would have liked the old one, too."

THE MOMENT TONY WRAPPED his arms around her, Lily tried to stiffen. She began to list in her mind all the reasons why she should back away. But even as she summoned them up, they streamed away. It felt so good just to lay her head against his chest and lean against him. His steady heartbeat lulled her. Unlike the other times he'd held her, there was no fire, no explosion of pleasure. All she felt was a sweet, spreading warmth. Oh, standing here felt much more than good. It felt just right. If anyone else had ever held her this way, she'd forgotten it, and she found herself wanting to stay right where she was, perhaps forever.

It was that thought that finally had her drawing back.

"I know just what you're going to say," Tony said, dropping his arms. "Time to get back to business." He hitched his head toward the door. "We'll take that run."

As he took her hand and drew her with him out the door, she wondered why she felt so let down.

"YOU'RE GOOD," Tony said, slowing as they neared the end of a path. And she was. After jogging the ten blocks to the park, they'd run for fifty minutes, or roughly four miles, at a steady pace. And in spite of the fact that his legs were longer, he hadn't had to slow his pace by much. "Let's walk for a bit."

"I should get back to the hotel. I want to translate my notes onto my laptop."

"First I'm treating you to lunch," Tony said, steering her to the entrance where a vendor was stationed. "And I'm not taking no for an answer. You can't come to New York and not sample some of our finest street cuisine. What do you take?"

"Hot dogs are not on my diet."

Tony threw back his head and laughed. "They're not on anybody's diet. They're probably lethal. Certainly, a mortal sin. That's why they're so good."

When she still hesitated, he said, "C'mon. You

wouldn't eat the breakfast I fixed you, and you're going to need your strength for that report. Just one hot dog. We'll split it.''

The vendor had already stuffed one into a roll and was poised to reach for condiments.

"If we pile enough stuff on it, we're bound to hit at least a few of the recommended food groups," he said.

A grin tugged at the corners of her mouth. "I'm beginning to understand for the first time how that snake in the Garden of Eden wore down Eve."

"I'll take that as a compliment. What do you want on it?"

"Mustard, onions and chili."

He grabbed her and kissed her hard on the mouth. "I think I love you. Tell me you play basketball and I'll buy a ring and propose."

"I think you're crazy," she said.

"Could be." Because he wanted very much to kiss her again, he dug his hand into his sweats and busied himself exchanging bills for the loaded hot dog. Then he nudged her back through the park entrance. "I've never met anyone who liked exactly what I like on my hot dog."

"It's a fluke. And you can forget about the ring. I don't play basketball."

"Bummer." The first few benches he spotted were taken. The sun that had finally made its appearance had lured Manhattanites in all shapes and sizes out of their apartments. A nanny pushed a stroller toward them while its occupant protested loudly. A dog-sitter passed them with three beagles and a miniature poodle in tow.

Spotting a large rock, he urged her onto the grass

and headed toward it. "There's a big game Sunday. The Murphys vs. the Romanos. Family pride is at stake, and we're short a player because Sam's wife is seven months pregnant."

"I can't—"

"You won't have to do anything but run up and down the court," he said as he gestured her down on the rock. "But we need a full team to intimidate the Murphys."

She narrowed her eyes. "Don't you ever take no for an answer?"

He grinned as he held the hot dog within an inch of her lips. "Not if I can help it. Try a bite."

She did, then closed her eyes to savor the mix of flavors. Watching the pleasure move across her face, he wanted to kiss her again.

"It's a good thing we're sharing," she said. "Otherwise, I'd have to eat grapefruit and tofu for a week."

"Grapefruit and tofu?" He shuddered. "That's awful."

She laughed, then took another bite when he offered it.

"I'm going to have to fix you a real meal."

She licked mustard off her thumb. "I thought Lucy was the cook."

"She's the most talented, but all the Romanos cook," he explained around a mouthful. "My brothers and I spent our formative years in the kitchen of Henry's Place. My father ran the hotel, but my mother ruled in the restaurant. We were her slaves. She even recruited my father at times. If we didn't do food prep or cook, we had to do the dishes."

"I spent a lot of time in the kitchen when I was growing up, too. Every time I made a mistake at the dinner table, my stepmother would banish me there."

"A mistake?" Tony asked.

"Spilled my milk or used the wrong fork. Pamela was always a stickler for proper etiquette."

"She must be a jerk, too."

Lily shrugged. "I'm learning to handle it."

Tony could see that she was. And she wasn't used to having anyone help her or even watch out for her. Tony found it hard to imagine what his own life might have been like without the solid support he'd always had from his family. He was about to tell her that she shouldn't have to handle everything on her own when a cell phone rang. Hers.

SHE DUG IT OUT of the pouch around her waist. "Sorry. It's probably my father." She took a second to brace herself. "Hello?"

"We've had a family meeting," Pamela said.

A family meeting. How like Pamela to phrase it that way. They'd had a family meeting that she hadn't been invited to.

"Your father and I will be in New York later today. You're not to do anything until then."

Lily felt her stomach sink, but she kept her voice steady. "That's not the agreement my father made with me an hour ago."

"Are you questioning my word?" Pamela asked.

Lily could hear surprise and anger in her tone and felt a little better. It wasn't easy to ruffle Pamela's control. "I'm merely asking to talk to my father."

"He's on another line."

"Put him on this one."

"Fine."

Lily counted three beats of silence and then her father said, "Lily, I don't have time for this. Jerry, Pamela, and I are in agreement, and Pamela and I will arrive in New York late tonight."

"I told you that I can handle this job. And we agreed—"

"There are certain things that Pamela has made me aware of. A lot is riding on this deal. Jerry informs me that Giles Fortescue is on the scene."

"What does Giles have to do with this?"

"You know you can't be trusted to think rationally around him. Expect Pamela and me in the morning. We'll handle everything from that point on."

"Dad, wait. I—" She broke off when she realized that he'd ended the call. For a second, she was tempted to throw the phone. Instead, she jammed it back into the pouch she'd taken it from.

"Does he always cut you off like that?" Tony asked.

"Yes." Because she couldn't sit still a moment longer, she rose and began to pace. "He never listens. He still thinks of me as the child I used to be—clumsy and incompetent." She found a pebble along the side of the path and gave it a kick. "This job. He promised it would be mine. It was my one chance to prove to him—and to Jerry and Pamela too—that I can be an asset to the company. Now, he's coming to handle it himself."

She didn't even know that he'd followed her until his hands gripped her shoulders and turned her. "The only McNeil I'm doing any business with is you."

"Oh." The anger that had bubbled up in her when her father had disconnected the call drained away, and taking its place was a warmth, sweet and solid. It occurred to her that she was losing ground fast with this man. Business and pleasure, it was all blurring together into one. Watching him now, seeing the understanding in his eyes, she could almost feel the earth shifting under her feet. In another moment, she would be tumbling into...*love?*

No. She'd tumbled into what she'd thought was love before, and it had been a disaster. What she felt for Tony was desire, and desire wasn't love. A smart woman didn't confuse the two.

A cell phone rang. His, she realized, as he dropped his hands from her shoulders and fished it out of his sweatpants. Saved by the bell. But she needed more than a bell. She needed a miracle. She'd come here to prove to her father that she could be an asset to McNeil Enterprises. To do that, she was supposed to deliver Henry's Place on a platter. It was bad enough that she was sleeping with Tony Romano. She could not, would not, fall in love with him. No way. It was not going to happen.

But as Tony talked on the phone, she couldn't prevent herself from sensing that old black cloud above her head again.

"YOU SAID YOU WANTED to know if Vera and I noticed anything suspicious."

As he listened to Alistair's voice in his ear, Tony wanted to curse. In the moment that it had taken him to fish out his phone, all of the worry and fear had returned to Lily's eyes. "What have you got?"

"A tall blond chap, midthirties, I'd say—and handsome if you fancy the Viking type as Vera does. He's been asking the staff a lot of questions, and he's pumping Vera now."

"Do you have a name?" Tony asked. He thought he might have one. The description fit the man who'd kissed Lily's hand in the lobby. Giles Fortescue.

"Negative on that. But Vera is looking into the crystal for him. She'll have it before she's done with him. Over and out."

The moment he put away the phone, Lily said, "I have to get back to the hotel."

He took one look at the determined set to her chin and said, "Okay. But why don't you tell me about your ideas for Henry's Place while we walk?"

"Because I don't have my notes typed up yet. And that's what I should be doing rather than sitting here in the park eating forbidden food."

When she moved onto the path, he fell into step beside her. "You can get back into one of your sexy business suits and make a formal presentation later. Just give me a little preview of what you're thinking. I swear I won't hold you to it if you want to make changes later."

She ran a hand through her hair. "Why do you want me to do this? I'm not fully prepared."

He began to tick his reasons off on his fingers. "Because I'm curious. Because it's a lovely day and I don't get out of the hotel as much as I'd like to, and if I distract you by asking you to talk business, I'm hoping that it will take us longer to walk back. Because if we talk business, I can write off the three bucks I spent on that hot dog."

She smiled then, and he saw some of the tension and worry ease.

"Last but not least, because I'll keep badgering you until you give in," he added.

"I think you're the most persistent man I've ever met," she said.

"Why fight it then?"

"My father would never approve. He trains all his executives to use handouts with charts and graphs."

"You can tell him I'm a very difficult client. I find it next to impossible to take no for an answer."

Turning, she narrowed her eyes and met his. "All right. But I don't want any complaints that you're bored when you have to sit through charts and graphs."

"Scout's honor."

She snorted. "Please. Don't expect me to believe that you were ever a Boy Scout."

But she didn't object when he took her hand as they left the park and joined the pedestrians walking down the Avenue of the Americas.

"If Henry's Place was yours, what changes would you make?" he asked.

"This won't be in any particular order. My experiences in Europe, specifically in France and Italy, taught me that there's a growing market for small hotels that operate like guest houses, offering personal service with great attention to detail. That's what I'd like to turn Henry's Place into. I'll begin with the biggest changes and work down to the smaller ones. First, I'd turn your father's penthouse into a restaurant, offering intimate dining with a view. Hotel guests would be given priority seating, but I would also open it to the public. Second, I have plans for the lobby."

As she continued to talk, Tony watched her warm to

her theme. There wasn't a doubt in his mind that she knew her business. What surprised him was that she clearly loved it—another indication that she wasn't the shark she wanted to be. When she started describing how she would turn the upper lobby into a destination for high tea complete with a string quartet, he could picture it in his mind.

"Then you would want to turn the main restaurant of the hotel into something with a distinct character," she said, "something a cut above the run-of-the-mill coffee shop. I'm thinking a French bistro or a pub."

"How about Italian food?" he asked. "Not the usual spaghetti and meatballs and pizza—but something a little more authentic and upscale? I've wanted to try something like that for years. Lucy would be in heaven if I let her create the menu."

"Sounds good. And then I have an endless list of little but important services."

"Such as?" Tony asked as he drew her around the corner onto Sixtieth.

She began to tap them off on her fingers. "Concierge services should be expanded to include a personal shopper. You should have an arrangement with a good health club so that you can provide passes for hotel guests. You should prepare a brochure with a map that illustrates different runs or walks that guests may take through the park."

"You are really very good at this," he said when she paused to take a breath. They'd stopped for a light, so he could see the flush that came to her cheeks that his words caused, the small flustered movement that she made with her free hand. Both reminded him that she wasn't used to hearing compliments. He was going to change that. "What's it going to cost me?"

"What?" She glanced up at him then.

"Bottom line—what would be the cost of making all the improvements you're talking about?"

"Well, I'd need to figure that out."

"How about a ballpark figure?"

Her eyes narrowed. "No. I can't pick a number out of the air for you. I have to calculate it—run some projections—all of which I could be doing right now back at the hotel. Besides, you'll need a five-year plan. That way you could start with one project and phase the others in."

"Come on, give me a hint."

She shook her head and turned her vibrant green eyes on him. "But let me get to my laptop and I'll put together the specifics."

The light changed. Pedestrians streamed past them. Tony was barely aware of the movement, he wasn't even sure that he could separate what Lily was saying into words anymore. He'd told her before that she was beautiful when she was smiling. He figured that on a scale of one to ten, she was only halfway there right now. Still, she was stopping his breath and wiping his mind as clean as a slate. It struck him then, right on the corner of a crowded Manhattan street, that he might be in danger of falling in love with Lily McNeil. His Goldilocks might be the one.

Ignoring the warning bells that were going off in the back of his mind, he reached out to trace a finger down her cheek "You know, you're beautiful when you—"

He broke off when he saw the expression in her eyes change to fear. She wasn't looking at him—but past his

left shoulder. He started to turn when she threw herself at him, hard, knocking him backwards. He
wrapped his arms around her while he tried to regain
his balance and failed. As they pitched backward,
landing hard on the sidewalk, he heard the crack of
noise. Even then, he might not have recognized it as a
shot, if he hadn't heard the bullet ping off metal.

Someone screamed, but the sound was nearly
drowned out by the squeal of tires and the roar of an
engine.

Tony tightened his arms around Lily when she tried
to raise her head. "Don't move," he ordered.

"He tried to shoot you," she said against his chest.
She was trembling now. "I saw the car. I saw the gun. I
can't...I can't breathe." He eased his hold on her. But
she was still gasping for air. "He...tried...to shoot...
you."

He sat up then and shifted her so that she was sitting
on his lap. "He didn't. Take deep breaths... There,
that's it." She was as white as a sheet, but she did just
what he told her. "Good job."

"You two all right?"

Tony stiffened as he glanced up to see that a small
crowd had gathered around them. But he focused on
the man who'd spoken. "Who are you?"

"I work for Sam," he said as he squatted down and
offered Tony the ID he'd already pulled out of his
pocket. "I was across the street from the hotel, and I got
a partial plate. It was a dark blue sedan, four doors."

Lily drew in a deep breath. "I got a good look at the
shooter."

"Sam was right," the man said. "You've got some
real trouble here."

7

LILY WOULDN'T HAVE BELIEVED that so many people could fit into the living room of the penthouse suite. Within twenty minutes of the time that she and Tony had arrived back at Henry's Place, the entire Romano family had gathered. In the overstuffed chair near the fireplace, Sam was working quietly on his laptop, while Tony leaned over his shoulder, a cell phone pressed to his ear. From what she'd been able to gather, Tony was trying to reach his cousin Nick to fill him in on what was happening. Behind Tony, his patience on a short leash, Drew paced back and forth, also talking into his cell phone.

Lily envied Drew the freedom. She would have been more comfortable pacing. Instead, she was trapped on the couch—with Grace to her left and Sam's very pregnant wife, A.J., on her right. Alistair, sketching on a pad, faced her across the narrow coffee table. Dame Vera sat at the end of the table, sipping sherry, engrossed in her crystal ball. The room itself was not large, but the three Romano men had clearly separated themselves from the women. Lily was almost sure it was because Sam and Drew didn't trust her. How could she blame them?

On the other hand, the women in the family were treating her like a hero because Tony had told everyone that she'd saved his life. She was even less comfortable with that.

Gina and Lucy had taken over the small kitchen and were dispensing food as quickly as it arrived on the dumbwaiter. Trays laden with the remains of crackers, meats, cheeses and fruit now lay scattered on tables throughout the room. Her own plate, which Tony had urged on her, lay untouched on the coffee table. She couldn't eat, not while the image of that gun pointed at Tony still lingered at the edges of her mind.

But the stress of drive-by shootings seemed to fuel the appetites in the Romano family. Lily didn't think she'd ever seen so much food disappear so quickly. She wasn't used to huge informal family meals where everyone talked and argued at once. Her own limited experience had been confined to sitting at a formal dining table with her father, her stepmother and stepbrother. She'd only been allowed to talk when she was specifically spoken to, and sooner or later, she'd never failed to breach at least one rule of etiquette. Then Pamela would banish her to the kitchen where the cook would try to cheer her up with ice cream or warm apple pie. Comfort food had turned her into a chubby, unhappy teenager.

Lily closed her eyes and drew in a deep breath. Her past no longer had to be her future. She could have whatever she wanted.

Except for Tony Romano. Slowly, she opened her eyes and looked at him. He wasn't looking at her. Since they'd arrived at the hotel, they'd had only a few moments alone together. Tony had used that to make sure she was all right. He hadn't seemed to be able to take her word for that. He'd run his hands over her, briefly, impersonally, and then he'd insisted on washing and bandaging the scrape on her elbow. By that time the Romanos had gathered, and chaos ensued.

She was fine. He was the one who'd almost been shot. Just as the image of that moment threatened to fill her mind again, Tony glanced up and met her eyes. For just a second she saw a mix of fury and frustration, so ripe that she could all but feel the heat of it across the room. Then as suddenly as if he'd turned a switch, those emotions were masked and he smiled at her. The warmth of that smile, lethal dimples and all, flowed through her, pushing away the fear.

It was in that instant that she made her decision. The first moment that she could snatch some time with him, she was going to tell him exactly why she'd come to his hotel. Then at least when her father arrived tomorrow, Tony would know what he was up against. Whatever the consequences to her career at McNeil Enterprises, she couldn't go on deceiving Tony or his family any longer.

"How does this look?" Alistair angled the sketch he'd been working on in Lily's direction.

Lily studied the drawing for a minute. The hairline was right, so was the chin, but something wasn't quite right. "The nose was broader, I think. I just got that one quick glimpse of him. I'm sorry I can't be more accurate."

"You're doing fine." A.J. patted her hand. "If someone had taken a shot at Sam, I don't think I could remember a thing."

"We're smart," Grace said. "We're going to figure out what's going on here. We just have to get all the facts on the table."

"Here! Here!" A.J. cheered. "I hear a future lawyer speaking. What do we know so far?"

Dame Vera set down the glass of sherry she'd been sipping. "The crystal is failing me today. There's deception on deception on deception. All I can see for sure is that it began on the Ides of March."

Grace grabbed a notepad from the table and jotted down 3-15. Lily felt the muscles of her stomach clench. Her birthday. Her fault?

Alistair glanced up from the sketch he was working on and rolled his eyes. "Vera, they need something more concrete than that."

Dame Vera sniffed. "In the *Thin Man* movies, William Powell didn't pay much attention to Myrna Loy, either. But she was usually right."

Lily's stomach clenched again.

A.J. glanced over at her husband, Sam. "Why don't you guys spill everything? You've been huddling over there mumbling to each other long enough. What do you know that you haven't told us?"

Sam's face softened into a slow grin before he shrugged and shifted his gaze from his wife to his two brothers. "What can I say? She's a damned good attorney. She can read people."

Drew fastened his gaze on Lily. "For starters, Tony has received two offers to buy the hotel, one from McNeil Enterprises the other from Fortescue Investments."

"Both of which I refused," Tony added smoothly.

"And the leak in the plumbing the other night wasn't the result of pipes rotting," Drew said. "Murphy says they were cut by an expert."

For the space of a beat, there was silence in the room, and Lily felt a ball of ice form in her stomach.

"You're saying it was deliberate sabotage?" Grace moved closer to the edge of the sofa.

"Sabotage?" Lucy echoed. "But why?"

Then everyone seemed to speak at once. By concentrating hard, Lily managed to pick up that Alistair and Dame Vera had turned over a sketch of the possible plumbing saboteur to Drew who'd identified him and was trying to run him to ground.

"We'll know more once I question him," Drew said, "but it's taking too much time. The license plate we got on the shooter will take time, too, because it's only a partial."

"Why would someone want to shoot Tony?" Lucy asked.

"Because they want the hotel, and Tony has refused to sell," Drew said, his gaze never leaving Lily. "With Tony out of the way, who would run this place?"

"I'm sure that Lucy could step into my shoes," Tony said. "And you all would pitch in to help her."

"We're assuming that Tony was the intended victim," Grace said. "But Lily was on that corner, too."

Tony's cell phone rang as A.J. managed to lean around Lily far enough to smile at Grace. "You're going to make a great lawyer. I should have thought of that. I think that pregnancy is destroying some of my brain cells."

"Who would want to shoot at me?" Lily asked. "No one knows I'm even here except my family. They wouldn't want to hurt me." But would they want to hurt Tony? Stunned that she would even think the

question, she recalled J.R.'s words. *This deal is crucial.*
She felt a chill run over her skin. No. It was ridiculous
to think that any member of her family would want to
harm Tony. She was just reacting to seeing him...to
seeing that shooter...

Grace patted her hand. "Tony's talking to my
brother, Nick. Before he became a lawyer, he was the
best P.I. in New York."

"Now, Sam's the best," A.J. said. "And Nick is a
proper Boston lawyer. But you can rest assured that
they'll figure things out."

Get a grip, Lily told herself. Her family wouldn't hurt
anyone just to get hold of a hotel. That was ridiculous.

WHEN SAM SIGNALED for the cell phone, Tony passed it
off to him. Nick and Sam were security experts. Between the two of them and Drew, he was certain that
they would beef up the security around the hotel even
more. Nick had been adamant that Sam should find
him a bodyguard, and Tony wasn't going to argue. He
was confident that he could find a way around one if
he needed to. The important thing was they had to
make sure that the family was safe. And he had to
make sure that Lily was safe.

The point that Grace had made had already occurred
to him. The shooter could just as well have been aiming
at Lily as at him. He still couldn't quite wipe from his
mind that instant when the shot had sounded and
she'd thrown herself against him. For one awful moment as they tumbled to the sidewalk, he'd believed
that she'd been shot.

Ruthlessly, Tony shoved the image away. He had to

keep his mind clear, his thoughts focused. Who and why? Until he found the answers to those questions, no one would be safe. For a few minutes, he let the conversation hum around him. Sam was consulting Drew, and with his brothers occupied, he could study the group at the other end of the living room.

Drew and Sam might still be keeping their distance, but his aunt and cousins and sister-in-law had rallied around Lily. In their minds, she'd saved his life. But he sensed that they also genuinely liked her. It occurred to Tony as he watched her lean closer to catch something Grace was saying that she looked right sitting there. Just right.

The realization hit him like a punch in the solar plexus. Lily McNeil was just right for him. If Drew hadn't chosen that moment to ask him a question, he might have laughed right out loud. He could almost hear his father's laughter in the room. Henry had always warned him that one day when he found a woman who felt just right, the task of convincing her of that wouldn't be easy. It had been part of his lecture that women were work.

At that moment, Lily glanced up and met his eyes. Slowly, irresistibly, desire moved through him, and with it came an ache—warm, throbbing and wonderfully new. He wanted her right then—more than he'd ever wanted her before. She might be out to get his hotel. He'd deal with that. Somehow. The one thing that he was sure of was that Lily McNeil was just right for him.

This time he was sure he heard his father's laughter echoing in the room.

EVERY TIME SHE LOOKED into his eyes, Lily felt the pull, as physically strong as if he had taken her hand and was drawing her toward him. Each time the sensation grew stronger. Each time she lost a little more of her will to pull away.

A.J. pulled a notebook out of her bag. "Assuming that Lily was the intended victim, let's make a list of suspects. Who knows you're staying here?"

Lily turned her attention to A.J. "My family and certain other people at the office—like my father's assistant. Someone from his office called to cancel my reservation here when they thought I was stuck in Tahiti."

"What about the tall blond Viking type who kissed your hand in the lobby this morning?" Dame Vera asked.

"I think his arrival was a coincidence," Lily said.

"He's been asking a lot of questions about the hotel. Alistair and I overheard him asking Lucy where Tony was going when he left with you for your run."

Lucy nearly dropped the plate she was clearing. "And I told him. I told him Tony was going to the park to run." Guilt-stricken, she turned to Tony. "He wanted to set up an appointment to talk with you. I didn't think."

Tony moved to Lucy and drew her close. "Why would you? I think we're getting a little paranoid here. We don't know for sure that the man in that car was shooting at either Lily or me."

"Is this the man?" Alistair asked, angling the sketch once more in Lily's direction.

Lily's eyes widened. "That's him. That's definitely him."

"Well, it's not the man who tampered with the pipes," Alistair commented.

"He doesn't look a thing like the Viking, either," Dame Vera said.

No, it certainly wasn't Giles, Lily thought. But as the Romanos crowded close to study Alistair's drawing, her mind was racing through the possibilities. Giles Fortescue had made an offer for Henry's Place, and he had somehow known that she was staying here. Did he have a spy at McNeil Enterprises? She couldn't imagine either her father or stepmother giving him that kind of information. And J.R. had not been happy to learn that Giles was registered at the hotel.

She couldn't actually be thinking that Giles would be involved in a drive-by shooting, could she?

But he'd known that she and Tony had gone to the park for a run.

"Anybody recognize him?" Drew asked the question of everyone, but once again his gaze was on Lily.

"No," she said.

"Who's the Viking?" Sam asked.

"He's Giles Fortescue, my ex-fiancé," Lily said.

"Well, there's a little fact we've been missing," Drew said. "When were you going to let us know that there's a jealous lover we can add to the mix?"

"Ex-lover." Tony laid a hand on Drew's arm. "I've known about him. So if you're annoyed, take it out on me."

Drew whirled on Tony. "She's blinding you. Can't you see—?"

"Let's take this outside, bro." Tony spoke in a very soft voice.

For a moment, a sizzling silence filled the room. During it, Sam tucked his laptop under his arm and moved to Drew's other side. Then, together, the three brothers left the suite.

TONY LED THE WAY around a row of terra cotta pots bursting with flowers to the edge of the basketball court. Usually it only took him a few minutes to get his temper under control, but he found that his hands and jaw were still tightly clenched when he turned to face his two brothers. He might have even thrown the first punch—something he'd trained himself not to do—but he had his wits about him enough to know that wouldn't solve the problem of keeping Lily safe.

Tony made himself take a deep breath. "What the hell is the matter with the two of you? Lily may very well have saved my life this afternoon. Whatever you think is going on, she's not involved."

Fury flashed in Drew's eyes. "She's up to her pretty little neck in it."

Sam placed a hand on Drew's arm. "He's not going to believe it until he sees it."

"Sees what?" Tony asked.

Sam moved to a nearby picnic table, opened his laptop and began punching keys. "I've had men working on this since you told me you'd been fielding offers for the hotel. I ran a check on McNeil Enterprises, much deeper than the one you asked me to run on Lily. Look what I found."

Tony looked over his brother's shoulder at the screen. What he saw didn't make any sense at first.

"It's a listing of all of McNeil Enterprises' subsidiary companies and their holdings," Sam explained. "Pay particular attention to Langford Properties. That subsidiary was formed two years ago. It's headed up by

Pamela Langford-McNeil, and it's become their New York City real estate acquisition arm. So far, they've been concentrating on one section of the city."

Even with Sam highlighting it on the screen for him, it took Tony a few minutes to see it. Then slowly as he read the street addresses, the significance began to sink in. Langford Properties currently owned the entire city block that Henry's Place sat on.

"When McNeil first approached you, what did he tell you?" Drew asked.

"He said that he was interested in acquiring a few small hotels on Manhattan and that he intended to put some money into renovations that would capitalize on their individual charm. He didn't mention that he'd bought out the whole block."

"What about Fortescue?" Sam asked.

"He called a week after McNeil did to say that he would beat any offer that McNeil gave me. I told him that Henry's Place was not for sale."

"But when the little blonde called, you agreed to let her move right into Dad's suite," Drew said.

"Drew." Sam's voice was sharp. "We came out here to talk. We're not going to get to the bottom of this if we start throwing punches."

Drew threw up his hands, palms out. "Okay. Okay, I'm sorry. For now."

Sam turned to Tony. "Why did you agree to see Lily?"

Because of her voice. It was the truth, but it was bad enough that he'd admitted that to himself. He certainly wasn't going to say that out loud to his brothers. If he didn't know her, didn't believe in her, he would probably have felt the same way. So he shoved his fisted hands in his pockets and gave them part of the truth. "She told me that she was heading up a new division of McNeil Enterprises. Since I had been firm about my decision not to sell, she wondered if I might be interested in her consulting services."

Drew made a sound, and Tony pinned him with one look. "She offered to take a look at the hotel, and then draw up a five-year plan for renovations."

"Free of charge," Sam said.

"That's right. But she wanted first shot at presenting a loan package that would finance the renovations. I figured the loan would be structured so that I wouldn't be able to pay it back on time—and then they'd foreclose."

"Good figuring," Sam said and sent a grin in Drew's direction. "See. He's not totally besotted."

"Yet," Drew grumbled.

"The loan deal might explain the sabotage," Sam continued. "Repairs like that would hike up the kind of money you'd need to borrow."

Drew shook his head in disgust. "You figured you were being suckered and you still agreed to see her?"

Tony shrugged. "I'm going to have to do renovations. I had Sam check Lily out, and her background is in small hotels that focus on individualized service. As I said before, I figured I could pick her brain. No harm done."

Sam closed down his laptop. "I keep telling Drew that you haven't entirely gone brain dead. The thing is—the loan scheme might explain the damage to the plumbing. But loans and foreclosures take time."

"But if they shoot me, there's at least a chance that

Henry's Place will go on the market right away," Tony said.

"Bingo," Sam said.

Drew frowned at both of them. "And she knew you were going to be in the park with her today. The consulting gig could just have been a way to get close so that she could set you up."

Tony took one step toward Drew before his brother held up both hands, palms out in a gesture of surrender. "This isn't going to work unless we brainstorm all the possibilities."

Because he was feeling the urge to punch Drew again, Tony bent down, picked up one of the basketballs that always lay along the edge of the court and began to bounce it. "Lily didn't set me up. And Grace made an excellent point. The shooter may have been aiming at Lily. That started me thinking. She wasn't even supposed to get here yesterday. Something happened to McNeil's company plane, and she was supposed to be stranded in Tahiti. Someone even called to cancel her reservation and her appointment with me. Maybe Lily wasn't ever supposed to get here." He tossed the ball to Sam. "Can you look into what happened to the plane?"

"I can try."

"While you're at it, check out Fortescue. Two years ago, Lily broke off the engagement and killed the merger plans between Fortescue and McNeil. He might have more than one reason to make sure she doesn't get a chance to lead me down the garden path."

"And you're sure she isn't doing just that?" Drew

asked as he caught a pass from Sam and began to dribble it toward the center of the court.

"She's not leading me anywhere I don't want to go," Tony said with a smile. And he hoped to hell that was true.

THE MOMENT THE THREE Romano men left the suite, Lucy raced to the window. "I've got five bucks that says Tony throws the first punch."

"My money's on Drew," Grace said. "He needs to work on that temper of his."

A.J. turned to Lily. "No one ever puts money on my man. But it's not that he's a coward."

Grace laughed. "He's the baby. He had to learn to be smarter and sneakier."

"We...I shouldn't let them fight. This is my fault," Lily said, trying to rise.

Grace and A.J. both clamped hands on her arms. "No. They'll sort it out."

Lily glanced from A.J. to the other women. "Do they do this often?"

Gina nodded. "It's worse when Nick's around. It's a testosterone thing."

"But this...this is my fault," Lily said.

"No," Gina said. "They're worried about their brother, and Tony's worried about you. They'll feel a lot better after they let off some steam."

"Crisis is over," Lucy reported from her vantage point at the window. "All bets are off. They've decided to settle their differences on the basketball court. I think it's safe to join them now."

"Sam will win," A.J. said.

"My money's on Tony," Grace said.

"I'll take Drew," Lucy said.

To Lily's surprise, the women rose then, with the exception of A.J. who needed Alistair's help to lever herself off the sofa. As she followed the others through the door, Lily's glance fell on the roses that Tony had left outside the room earlier, and she remembered Giles and his invitation to have drinks with him. A glance at her watch told her that she had thirty minutes to meet him at the Waldorf-Astoria. If Giles was behind the sabotage and the shooting, she wasn't going to have a better chance to pump him for answers.

"Aren't you going to join us and watch the game?" Dame Vera asked.

Startled, Lily turned to find Dame Vera right behind her. "I have something I need to take care of. I'll be along in a few minutes."

To her surprise and dismay, Vera raised a hand and rested it on her cheek. "You're worried that your family has something to do with the troubles."

"No." But wasn't that why she was going to see Giles—so that she could assure herself that he was behind the problems and not her family? Then she blurted out, "I'm afraid that I might have brought the problems here. My birthday is on the Ides of March."

"Be very careful, my dear. Make sure you meet him in a public place."

Lily felt her skin crawl as Dame Vera swept through the door. Could the woman actually read minds?

As Sam stepped up to the foul line, Tony shoved sweat out of his eyes and concentrated on drawing in deep breaths. He'd fouled his brother on purpose so that he could get some oxygen into his lungs. The block that

Drew had thrown him when Tony had taken his first shot was still causing his breath to hitch. The problem about playing basketball to vent your anger and frustration was that the first ten minutes were brutal. It had taken him that long to realize that Lily hadn't followed the other women out to the court.

He'd shoved that first quick spurt of panic down, telling himself that he was overreacting. She was in the penthouse where no one could get to her. And he could hardly leave the court to check on her with his two brothers rushing him.

The length of time Sam was dribbling told him that his brother was winded, too. So was Drew, if the way he was bent over his knees was any indication. A quick glance at his watch told him that Lily had been in the penthouse alone for nearly half an hour. This time he wasn't so quick to ignore the panic. What was she doing in there? Had she been more hurt than she'd let on? He'd taken her down with him pretty hard when that shot had gone off.

Sam tossed the ball up with one hand and it whooshed through the basket. Drew grabbed it as it fell, but Tony threw a block that left his brother on his backside before he snatched the ball, tore down the court and scored.

"Time out," he called as his brothers thundered past him in a heated contest for the rebound.

"Chicken," Sam said.

Tony grinned, but his gaze was already shifting to the penthouse. "Somebody had to call it. I think I have a cracked rib."

"Good game." A.J. was the first to arrive from the

edge of the court. "Thanks for calling it," she murmured in a low voice as she passed Tony.

The way Gina, Grace and Lucy were congratulating Drew told Tony who had won the game. "I want a recount," he called to them.

"Your mind wasn't on the game," Sam said, between breaths. "Next time we'll have to double team him or he'll be impossible."

"Deal," Tony said, already moving toward the penthouse. Lily was probably working on her presentation. He certainly hadn't given her any time to prep it. Or she might be on the phone with her father. He quickened his pace.

Dame Vera stepped into his path. "She's gone."

This time the panic was a sharp slice in his gut. "Where?"

But he knew even before Vera said, "To meet the Viking."

He was cursing himself as he strode toward the penthouse door. Of course, she'd gone to meet Giles Fortescue. He'd seen the note, the flowers. He should have known she'd go to the Waldorf-Astoria to meet him.

The problem was he wasn't thinking clearly. He hadn't been thinking clearly since he'd first heard Lily McNeil's voice over the telephone.

LILY DIDN'T spot Giles until she'd climbed up the stairs leading to the lobby of the Waldorf-Astoria and turned. The moment she did, a sense of déjà vu streamed through her. The lobby bar was located up another short flight of stairs. He looked just as striking as ever. There were flowers on the table—roses in a cut crystal vase. He would have ordered them specially. As she climbed the steps, she caught their scent mingling with burning candles. Nearby, champagne chilled in a silver bucket, and next to it was a box of chocolates. The table where he sat was secluded, set near a window overlooking the street. He would have taken care in the selection, slipping the hostess an extra tip for securing just the right spot.

The scene was so typically Giles that it nearly made her smile. He'd always given her roses and chocolates. The gifts had made her feel special, but she suspected now that he'd probably given the same gifts to any woman he dated.

The roses he'd sent to the penthouse had made her angry. Angry at herself. For the past two years she'd blamed herself for being so gullible. But she wasn't that same girl anymore. Now she found the predictability of the scene almost amusing.

But she didn't have time for either amusement or anger this evening. She'd come here on a mission. During the time she'd taken to dress and sneak out of the hotel, she'd been thinking. Hard. There had to be some reason that both Fortescue Investments and McNeil Enterprises were so interested in Henry's Place. Perhaps something that might make it worth someone's while to eliminate Tony Romano. Just the thought had a chill moving through her. For tonight, she had to put fear aside too. She had to focus on getting information. Giles just might know why her father was so desperate to get hold of the hotel.

As she wove her way toward the table, Giles rose and moved to greet her. She could have sworn that the smile on his face was genuine.

"I wasn't sure you'd come," he said as he drew back her chair and settled her in it.

He would have been sure two years ago. The fact that he wasn't now pleased her. "You went to a lot of trouble for a date who might not show up."

"Hope springs eternal."

She glanced around the room. A table to their right held two women, and closer to the bar, there was another group of women. "I don't suppose it would have taken you very long to find a replacement."

"Ouch." He tipped champagne into their glasses. As they sampled it, he studied her over the rim of his glass. After a moment, he sighed. "You've changed. I could see the surface differences in the lobby this morning, but I can sense deeper ones now. You're not the naive young woman I romanced two years ago." He gestured toward the flowers and chocolate, and a glint of amusement came to his eyes. "This time around, you're going to see through all of this. And I'm not going to get you back, am I?"

She laughed then. Giles had always had an ability to laugh at himself. It was part of his charm. "You don't really want me back. We wouldn't suit at all."

"I suppose not. But a man can have regrets."

Her eyes narrowed as she studied him. He looked much the same as he had when she'd first met him and taken that initial heady tumble into what she'd thought was love. The blond hair, the chiseled features, the intense, dark blue eyes that had made her believe she was the only woman in the room. In the world. Suddenly, Lily didn't feel quite so stupid anymore. Giles Fortescue was a man who would go to any woman's head. The problem was that he *did* go to a lot of women's heads, and he enjoyed that so much that he would never settle down with one. Two years ago when he'd admitted that to her, she'd blamed it on something lacking in herself.

"So if it wasn't my charm that drew you here, why did you come?" Giles asked.

The other thing she'd liked about Giles was that he was smart. For a moment Lily debated whether or not to tell him the truth. If he was somehow involved in the plumbing sabotage or the shooting...

"Pardon me, sir."

Lily glanced up to see a waitress standing at the table with a note on her silver serving tray.

"One of the ladies at the bar asked me to deliver this."

"Thank you." Giles gave it a quick glance before tucking it into his pocket.

Smiling, Lily shook her head. Giles Fortescue was definitely a ladies' man. And a shrewd businessman. But a saboteur or a killer? She didn't think so. Leaning toward him, she said, "I'll try to be brief. One question before I begin. Why did you really ask me to come here?"

He leaned back in his chair and sipped champagne. "One of the things I always liked most about you was your intelligence."

"That's not an answer."

His grin was rueful. "I was going to lead up to my hidden agenda—maybe halfway through the bottle of champagne."

"Now would be good. The love of your life may be waiting at the bar."

He laughed then, and in a quick gesture, took her

hand and raised it to his lips. "I really do have regrets, you know. More with each passing minute. And I told you the truth in the lobby this morning. I came to see you. I learned that you would be at Henry's Place on company business, and I wanted to meet up with you."

She frowned at him. "How did you find that out?"

"I called the office and spoke with Pamela. She told me that I could look you up here. She always regretted that you broke off the engagement."

Lily nodded to herself. That much made sense. Only *regret* wasn't the word that she would have chosen. Fury was the label she would have given to her stepmother's reaction. Control had always been Pamela Langford-McNeil's forte, but she'd nearly lost it when she'd found out that there would be no wedding. "I don't believe you flew across the country just to see if you could win me back. What was your other reason?"

"Okay." He raised both hands, palms out. "But this isn't the way I'd planned on leading up to it. So you have to promise that you won't give me an answer tonight. You'll take at least a few days to think about it?"

Lily stared at him. "Okay."

"I want to hire you away from McNeil Enterprises. I can offer you a vice president's position at Fortescue Investments."

For a moment, Lily couldn't say a word. Whatever she'd expected when she'd asked Giles the question, it wasn't this.

"You should see yourself. You look shell-shocked," Giles said. "For that reason alone, you ought to take my offer."

"Why would you want me at Fortescue?"

Giles made an impatient sound. "Because you're

good. I've checked into what you did while you worked for the Marchmount Hotel chain. Your father should have offered you a vice presidency as soon as you returned to his company. They don't value you enough at McNeil."

He looked sincere. But she remembered that Giles was a master at that. And he wasn't telling her the whole story. Lily was sure of it. "Are you looking for some leverage so that you can propose another merger to my father?"

Something flickered behind his eyes. "Perhaps. But that needn't concern you. The offer is genuine, and you can hire some attorneys to help write the contract so that a merger doesn't affect your position with the new company." He shrugged. "And if you eventually want to go back to McNeil, a few years with a vice presidency at Fortescue under your belt will make you very attractive to them."

He was right. She couldn't argue with the logic of his proposal. But she also couldn't let his offer distract her. She leaned back in her chair. "I'll think about it."

"Good." He topped off both of their glasses. "Now it's your turn to come clean. Why did you really join me here tonight?"

"I have some questions, and I think you might have a few of the answers."

"Ask away."

"Is Fortescue Investments interested in buying Henry's Place?"

His eyes narrowed then, and it wasn't amusement she saw, but speculation. "Why would you think that?"

"Because I know that you made Tony an offer, and

now you're here and you're questioning the staff about the hotel."

Giles sipped his champagne. "Okay. I'll admit I had another reason for coming here. Fortescue is interested in acquiring a string of small hotels in the New York City area, and Henry's Place heads the list." He met her eyes steadily. "But the job offer is genuine. I want you at Fortescue."

"Why is Henry's Place so attractive to you?"

"Three reasons. Location, location, location. It's close to the theater district, Central Park, and it's only fifteen blocks or so to prime shopping." Then the glint of amusement appeared again in his eyes. "Plus, Fortescue and McNeil are old rivals. We often go after the same property."

That made sense. But once again, Lily was sure he wasn't telling her everything. The guarded look in his eyes made her suspect that beating out McNeil Enterprises was why he was really interested in Henry's Place. Could the old rivalry between the two companies explain why her father was so desperate to get Tony Romano's hotel?

Or was there something going on that she didn't know about? Something that would tempt someone to get rid of Tony? She doubted very much that the hotel could continue to function without Tony. The rest of the Romanos had other careers, other priorities. Lucy wasn't nearly ready to take it over yet. Nor did she probably want to.

Lily took a quick sip of champagne to ease the fear that had lodged in her throat. "Someone wants very much to get hold of that hotel. Enough to cut some of the pipes last night and today someone tried to shoot

Tony. You wouldn't know anything about that, would you?''

She was almost sure it was surprise that flashed into Giles's eyes before they became guarded and a frown appeared on his forehead.

"Someone shot at him?"

Her reply was interrupted by the waitress who appeared carrying another note on a small silver tray. The flash of annoyance on Giles's face didn't prevent him from reaching for it. Lily was amused to see that this one required a reply. Her eyes rested for a minute on his hands as he picked up a pen—the long fingers, the meticulously manicured nails, the soft palms. Giles's gestures when he made them were smooth and calculated just as his lovemaking had been. She thought of Tony's hands—strong and just a bit rough. And his gestures—she'd have to describe them as spontaneous, genuine—just as his lovemaking had been. Giles had waited three months to take her to bed. Tony hadn't even waited until they'd introduced themselves. *Early to bed, early to rise...*

The little rhyme chanting in her head rekindled the memory of the first night she'd spent with Tony, and before she could prevent either, she felt her lips curve and heat stain her cheeks. Both sensations drew her back to where she was and what she'd come to do— pump Giles for information.

While Giles continued to write a response to his admirer, Lily glanced out the window. Rush-hour traffic had thinned a bit, but it was still moving in sudden and unpredictable fits and starts. She saw in it a metaphor for her conversation with Giles. She'd made some progress with him. Maybe. Did she really expect him to admit to her that he'd hired someone to take a shot at Tony? Did she really believe that the suave, urbane man sitting across from her had done something like that? Or did she only want to believe it because if Giles wasn't behind the sabotage and the shooting, the finger of suspicion would point to her family?

Her gut instinct told her that Giles lacked the passion to commit murder. He'd certainly lacked any kind of passion in their relationship. Looking back, she realized that his every move had been as smooth and calculated as this carefully orchestrated little rendezvous that he'd arranged right here at the Waldorf-Astoria.

Directly below her, a taxi nearly nicked another car as it wedged itself a place at the curb. Behind the vehicle, a blue sedan slammed on the brakes to keep from rear-ending the cab. She wondered if she would ever get used to New York City traffic.

The moment she realized the direction her thoughts had taken, she stiffened. Where had that stray little fantasy come from? McNeil Enterprises' main office operated out of San Francisco. She wasn't thinking, she couldn't be thinking of moving to New York City. Whatever she had going with Tony Romano was not only spontaneous, but it was *temporary*. *Fleeting* might be a better word. The affair would end when she told him the truth about why she'd really come to Henry's Place. And she was going to do that as soon as she got back to the hotel.

On the street below, a man unfolded himself from the back seat of the taxi. Tony. She knew before he even glanced up at the window. Icy ribbons of fear moved through her, and questions flooded her mind. How had he known she was here? She'd slipped out of the back of the hotel and walked three blocks before she'd hailed a taxi.

Dame Vera. Had she told Tony?

Unless...had Giles let him know? Could this whole elaborate rendezvous have been a trap to get Tony here?

8

"HEY, BUDDY. You owe me seven fifty."

Swearing under his breath, Tony whirled back to the taxi and shoved a fifty into the driver's waiting hand. "I want you to go around the corner and wait for me on the side street."

Fear had become a rusty claw in his gut. Of the three Romano brothers, he had the longest fuse. Usually, he controlled his temper by taking a rational approach. But there was nothing rational about what he felt for Lily. Despite Sam's assurances that Lily had been followed. Despite everything, Tony hadn't been able to convince himself that she was safe. He was nearly running as he entered the revolving door and pushed his way into the lobby. Then he took the stairs two at a time.

When Tony saw her, the fear washed away in the flood of new emotions slamming into him.

She was standing, her palms flat on the table, leaning towards Giles Fortescue. The first thing that registered in his mind was the dress—it was black and it covered a minimal amount of skin. His first thought when he could manage one was that she was wearing it for Giles Fortescue. Never mind that the man sitting across from her at the table couldn't see her legs—which were nothing short of miraculous. Every other man in the bar—including the one Sam had assigned to follow her—could see them.

In a desperate attempt at control, Tony tried to identify the emotions swirling through him.

Jealousy was easy to identify. But he'd never known it to burn like a red-hot flame in his gut. Every little detail—flowers, candlelight gleaming off a silver champagne bucket—added fuel to the fire.

Lust. Oh, yeah, there was that, too. Never mind that caveman tactics had never been his style. Right now, he had an overwhelming urge to just throw Lily over his shoulder and cart her out of the room.

And bubbling up, fighting for equal time with the jealousy and the lust, was anger. He was furious with himself. How in the world had he ever gotten himself into a situation where one woman could have this kind of power over him?

He wanted to grab her. He wanted to punch Giles Fortescue. It took almost more effort than he possessed to slow his steps and take a deep calming breath. The woman was driving him crazy. And it was only then as he stopped a few feet from the table that he was able to focus on the scene in progress.

Lily slammed a hand on the table, then leaned forward until her nose was inches from Giles's. "I'm only going to say this one time. If anything happens to Tony Romano and if I find out you're responsible, I'll personally...I'll personally make you pay."

"Lily, I assure you," Giles lifted both hands, and Tony could have sworn that one of them shook a bit, "I'm not a violent man. You know that."

"What I know," she said between gritted teeth, "is that someone is desperate to get their hands on

Henry's Place and you're on the list of suspects. For all I know, this whole meeting was just a charade to get Tony out of the hotel so that he would be vulnerable. I never should have come here."

"You're being irrational."

She leaned closer. "As long as I'm being clear."

Giles inched back in his chair a little. "Yes. You're clear as crystal. But I'm not the one who's trying to hurt Tony Romano."

"Consider yourself warned." Then she whirled to Tony and grabbed his arm. "C'mon, we're getting out of here."

Tony had time to see a flustered Giles rise to his feet and extend a hand. "Mr. Romano, Giles Fortes—"

The rest of the name was lost because of the speed at which Lily was pulling him through the bar. It occurred to him that this was what it might feel like to be thrown over someone's shoulder and dragged off. The thought made his lips twitch, and for the first time since he'd learned that Lily had left the penthouse, his tension eased.

"You scared the life out of me," she said as she urged him down the stairs. "I never would have left the hotel if I'd known you were going to follow. You shouldn't have. How did you know where I'd gone?"

"I read the card that came with the flowers," he said when she paused.

She spared him one angry glance before she shoved him into the revolving door and then wedged herself in next to him. "Isn't that a federal offense?"

"I didn't see a postage stamp on it." For some reason, probably because he had truly gone around the bend, Tony was beginning to enjoy himself.

Out on the street, she pulled him to a stop beneath the awning of the hotel. "What were you thinking?" She poked a finger into his chest. "Someone took a shot at you this afternoon. You should never have left the hotel. Someone could have followed you here. This could have been a trap." She waved a hand in the direction of the street. "They could be out there right now—just waiting for a chance to—"

A blast from a horn drowned out her next few words. With the setting sun in her hair and fury in her eyes, she was beautiful. Later he would wonder why it struck him so hard right then. Even later, he would blame it on the fact that his mind had finally snapped. But right now all he could think was that she looked like some avenging angel who was determined to rescue him. And he was delighted with her. Each thought she put into words was an echo of exactly what he'd intended to tell her. But right now, all he wanted to do was one thing. He grabbed her, pulled her close and covered her mouth with his.

Oh, it was a mistake. He knew that. And he'd meant to keep the kiss brief—just one sample that would last him until they were someplace safe and private. But the moment that her taste poured into him, he could feel his last thin grip on reality and sanity begin to stream away as quickly as chalk drawings on a rain-washed sidewalk.

And then he didn't think at all. Oh, in some vague corner of his mind, he was aware that pedestrians passed them on the street, and at least one gave a long, low wolf whistle. But the noises were just a buzz in his head. Her hands slid up his back to pull him closer, urging him to take what he wanted. And what he wanted was to explore every inch of her. The hunger that she ignited in him went from spark to flash fire in an instant. He should have been worried that they were on the street, exposed. But that warning voice was more background noise, muted, almost indecipherable as his mind narrowed to Lily.

Lily. He had to touch her. It had been too long. He drew his hand down her side to her hip and pressed her closer. The way she fit against him was so right. And her taste. He'd been craving that wild, sweet flavor—but each time he sampled it, there seemed to be something new, something that pulled him deeper and deeper. And there at last was the deep rich taste of her need. It was the echo of his own, and he knew that he would never get enough of it.

Far away came the sound of tires screeching, horns blasting. He was standing on a New York City sidewalk. In some dim corner of his mind the sounds reminded him of that fact. But the ground beneath his feet wasn't solid. He could have sworn that the world was tilting and he was falling....

It was the quick skip of fear that tightened his thin grip on reality. Fear of what Lily made him feel. Head swimming, he swore under his breath and gathered the strength to pull away. Somehow, he'd moved her so that she was against the wall of the building. He had no idea how they'd gotten there. Worse, he was almost sure he was trembling.

THE MOMENT HE RELEASED HER, Lily surfaced slowly. Sensations came first. Her skin felt hot and icy cold at the same time. She pressed her fingers to her lips. They were vibrating. She was sure of it. And her heart. She flattened her other hand against her chest to keep it from pounding its way right out of her. Only then did she become aware that she couldn't feel her legs. If her back hadn't been pressed against the brick wall of a building, she might have slipped right to the sidewalk when Tony dropped his hands and stepped back.

Because she couldn't trust herself to move, or speak—she was pretty sure her lips weren't yet capable of forming words—she simply stared at him. His mouth had flattened to a grim line. She didn't let her gaze linger there because just looking made her want the pressure of his mouth against hers again. His hair was mussed, and her palms still tingled from the sensation of running her hands through it. She wanted to run them through it again.

She wanted him.

The realization struck her in a blinding flash. Not just physically—though there was that too. She wanted the whole package—the man who could turn her brains to mush with a kiss or even a look. The man who would stand at her side and defend her, even if it meant going against his brothers.

The horrible thing was, she wanted him more than she wanted to get her father's approval, more than she wanted to take her place at McNeil Enterprises, more than anything.

And she wasn't going to be able to get him. Once he found out her real agenda for coming to Henry's Place, he was going to hate her.

A horn blasted on the street, and several others echoed it.

Tony swore under his breath.

It was only then that she noticed the fury in his eyes. But she hadn't tasted any anger in his kiss.

"C'mon," he said, grabbing her hand and heading toward the corner. "I paid my taxi driver to wait for us around the corner. I thought that would be safer than flagging one down in front of the hotel."

"You're angry," she said, increasing her pace to keep up with him.

"At myself," he said. "I'm not taking very good care of you. I should have anticipated that you'd come here. He sent you flowers, set up a romantic tryst. Any woman in her right mind would have been flattered."

"Flattered?" She stopped short as they turned the corner, and waited until he was facing her. "You can't think I came here because of that."

"Why did you? Are you still in love with him?"

"No. I met with him to find out if he knew anything about that shooter this afternoon."

Tony stopped to stare at her. "You thought he'd just spill everything?"

"No. But I wanted to see his face when I told him about the shooting. I also wanted to find out if he knew anything about why…" she hesitated, then said, "why someone is so desperate to get hold of your hotel that they'd try to get rid of you."

"Sam and Nick are checking into that."

Lily's stomach clenched and she prayed that whatever they might find out would not involve her family. "Good. But Giles is in the business. I thought he might know something."

"Did he?" Taking her arm, Tony drew her around the corner.

People had begun to trickle out of the row of brownstones that lined the street. Many of them had been converted into small office buildings. As Tony steered her around a group of strollers, she gathered her thoughts. ''Maybe. He's very smooth—and smart. And I can't say that I've got a history of reading him very well. But he made me a job offer.'' Pausing for a moment, she frowned. ''There's always been a rivalry between Fortescue Investments and McNeil Enterprises. Giles admitted that influenced his offer. He also admitted to wanting to get even with McNeil Enterprises because my father reneged on the merger two years ago. But there could be a third reason. If Giles thought I might have any influence with you, he might want me at Fortescue just so he could get his hands on Henry's Place. My father...''

Breaking off, Lily bit down hard on her lower lip. She'd been about to say that her father was desperate to get his hands on Henry's Place. Guilt tightened the knots that had already formed in her stomach.

Dame Vera's words came back to her—''deception on deception on deception.'' That was why the woman hadn't been able to get a clear picture in her crystal. And how could she expect Tony to get a real handle on what was going on unless she told him everything?

''Tony, I—''

He cut her off by gripping her shoulders and turning her towards him. The fury was back, but it was banked. ''He could also want revenge on you for breaking off the engagement. A man with that kind of ego wouldn't like to be dumped. That shooter could have been aiming at you just as well as me.''

Still frowning, Lily shook her head. ''Giles just

doesn't have the passion for murder. Besides, it's been two years.''

"You know what they say about revenge. It's a dish best enjoyed when it's cold.'' Linking his fingers with hers, Tony drew her back into the flow of pedestrians.

"Or as much as I might hate to give him any credit, the man may simply be brilliant." He waited until she glanced up to meet his eyes, then continued, "He may have realized what an asset you'll be to Fortescue Investments. If I were in his shoes, that's all the motivation I'd need to hire you away from McNeil."

Lily merely stared at him as he raised their joined hands to his lips and brushed his mouth over her fingers. "You don't value yourself half enough," he murmured.

Warmth spread through her, thick and sweet as honey—along with another quick stab of guilt. He didn't know the real Lily. It was time he did. "There's something else I have to tell you."

"Let's get in the taxi first," he said as he drew her toward the curb. "I think we've tempted fate enough."

Lily spotted a cab sitting in a delivery space, about twenty yards away and across the one-way street. The moment the traffic cleared, Tony led her between two parked cars. She caught the movement out of the corner of her eye. By the time they'd taken two steps into the street, the car's motor was racing and it was hurtling toward them.

Fear filled her in a flash so bright that it numbed her. She couldn't seem to move.

"Run."

She wasn't sure if she'd shouted the word or if Tony had. But an arm clamped around her and her feet left the pavement. They were moving then, but so was the car. And it was faster. Much faster. A roaring filled her ears. The car was too close, the other side of the street too far. No time. Images bulleted into her mind, blurring together. A parked car blocking their path. The blue car, nearly upon them. A bald man with sunglasses behind the wheel.

Tony's arm banded her waist and they were airborne. An instant later, they smacked down hard on the hood of the parked car. Her body barely had time to absorb the impact before the car jolted. Metal screeched against metal. Then she was rolling with Tony onto the sidewalk.

TONY TWISTED to take the impact as they hit the cement. Before the pain had even had time to register, he leapt to his feet, dragging Lily with him. He was in time to see the blue car careen around the corner. Pedestrians scattered, horns blared. If he'd been alone, he would have run after it, chased it down. As it was, he was content to leave that job to the man Sam had assigned to follow him. He didn't want to leave Lily. He couldn't. He folded her into his arms and held her close. The coppery taste of fear was still lodged at the back of his throat.

"Are you all right?" he asked as he ran his hand up her back to the nape of her neck.

She nodded against his chest, but she didn't move except to tighten her arms around him. Neither did he. For the moment, he needed to be held. It had been too damn close. The scene kept replaying itself in his mind in one continuous loop. The car had been inches away when he'd tightened his grip on her and vaulted onto the hood of the car. Another second and...

Lily ran her hands up his back, and he felt his tension begin to ease. Each time he held her this way, it felt more and more—natural. Just right. He was going to have to give that some thought. Just as soon as he figured out who was trying to kill her. Or him. Or both of them.

"C'mon," he said, finally drawing back. But he kept his arm around her. "We're going back to Henry's Place and we're both going to stay there until we have this figured out."

"Good plan," Lily said as they walked along the sidewalk toward the still-waiting taxi.

LILY STARED into the bathroom mirror. Her damp hair was slicked back from her face and all she was wearing was a towel. Without the new hairdo and makeup, she looked very much like the old Lily. Despite two years of hard work and a seven-day success seminar in Tahiti, had she really changed at all?

Her own personal test of that was approaching with the speed of a runaway train. Just as soon as she toweled her hair and dressed, she was going to walk into the living room of the penthouse suite and tell Tony the truth about why she'd come to Henry's Place. She'd postponed that long enough.

But first she wanted to reassure herself that she hadn't changed back into the old Lily—the Lily who cut and ran when the going got tough. She pressed a hand against her stomach where the old familiar knots had formed. Deep inside of her, she felt the same way she had when she was ten and she'd run out of her fa-

ther's office with his laughter ringing in her ears. Truth
told, she'd felt pretty much the same way when she'd
informed Giles that she wasn't going to marry him.
Unable to face her stepmother's wrath or her father's
disappointment, she'd run away that time too.

It had occurred to her during her shower—which
had lasted so long, her skin had crinkled—that she was
about to repeat an old pattern. When she'd run out on
the wedding, she'd ruined everything that her father
and McNeil Enterprises had worked for two years to
arrange. What she was going to do in a few minutes
would ruin everything that McNeil Enterprises was
hoping for again. She doubted that Tony would be interested in doing any further business with her father
once she told him how she'd lied to him from the get-
go.

She sank onto the toilet and dropped her head into
her hands. Making love with Tony Romano had made
her lose her focus. From that moment on, the goal that
she'd been visualizing in her mind had begun to blur
and change until all she could think of was Tony. All
she could want was Tony. If she just hadn't crawled
into that bed with him.

No. She sat up and straightened her shoulders. The
one thing that she couldn't regret was everything she'd
shared with Tony.

But he would surely regret it. She stared at the bathroom door. When she worked up the courage to walk
through it, she was going to lose everything she'd ever
wanted—her father's approval, any chance she had of
a vice presidency at McNeil Enterprises, and she was
also going to lose Tony.

And that damned motivational guru in Tahiti had

made it sound so simple. Lily sighed as she toweled her hair and then pulled on sweats. She'd put it off long enough. When they'd gotten back to the hotel, the family had gathered in the penthouse again to get their assignments. Drew was running the license plate of the blue sedan. The man Sam had assigned to Tony had gotten it when he'd run after the car. She'd been able to tell them that it was the same car and the same man who'd taken a shot at Tony earlier in the day.

Tony was still insisting that she could be the intended victim—but no one was really buying into that theory. It just didn't make sense. Sam, Nick and his wife, Tyler, were all digging into what might make Henry's Place such a "desirable" property. Dame Vera was gazing into her crystal ball. But the end result of their hour-long meeting had been that they still didn't have a clue as to why someone would want to hurt Tony or her or both of them.

The least she could do was clear away one layer of the "deceptions" that were clearly leading to disasters. Straightening her shoulders, Lily opened the bathroom door, but she stopped short the moment she saw Tony sitting on the side of the bed. Her throat went dry and all the knots in her stomach tightened.

"Hi," he said as he slid from the bed and held out his hand. "I've got a surprise for you."

She moistened her lips and ignored his hand. "No. First, there's something that I have to tell you."

His brows lifted. "It won't wait."

She shook her head, and made herself keep her eyes on his. "I should have told you sooner. I—I came here under false pretenses." She cleared her throat. "I lied to you. There's no new division in McNeil Enterprises that offers consulting services to hotels. When you refused my father's offer to sell Henry's Place, he sent me here to spy on you, to discover anything that he could use to force you to sell."

"And the plan you outlined for me earlier? That was a lie too?"

"No. The plan is solid. But McNeil Enterprises never had any intention of offering you a financial package. So—that part of it was a lie."

There. She'd said it. Confession was supposed to be good for the soul, but it hadn't make her stomach feel any better. Tony's expression hadn't changed since she'd started her little speech. And now the silence had gone on for so long that it seemed to be a physical presence in the room. Why didn't he say something?

"Well? Aren't you going to say anything?" she asked.

"It took a lot of courage for you to tell me that," he said.

She stared at him. He should be angry, but there was no sign of it in his voice or in his eyes. His hands were hanging loosely at his sides—no clenched fists, no white knuckles. She took a step toward him. "What's wrong with you? I just told you that I came here to trick you and to take your hotel away from you. You don't look angry. You don't even look surprised."

He moved toward her then and tucked a strand of hair behind her ear. "When you first called, I figured that's pretty much why you wanted to come here."

"I don't understand...if you suspected that, why did you agree to see me?"

He smiled. "Your voice. The first time I heard it I wanted to meet you."

Frowning, she stepped back from him and gave her head a little shake to clear it. He had to be teasing with her, toying with her. "I can understand that you want revenge, and you have a perfect right to—"

"I'm telling you the truth, Lily. I'm not a stupid man, and my father told me once never to trust McNeil Enterprises. I suspected from the start that you came here with an agenda that would force me to sell Henry's Place to your company. But I wanted to meet you. It was just that simple. Oh, I told myself that I had my own agenda. I even had Sam run a check on you, and I was impressed with what you'd done when you worked for the Marchmount chain in Italy and France. I don't have your kind of education and background, your insight into what changes I could make to turn Henry's Place around. I tried to tell myself that was why I invited you. But I think it was your voice."

Oh, how she wanted to believe him. With every pore in her being she wanted the look in his eyes to be sincere. She wanted to trust that for some reason he didn't hate her. But...

"You don't believe me," he murmured. Somehow his hand had moved to the back of her neck.

She wanted to. More than that, she wanted to move toward him, feel his arms go around her, to lose herself in him. "This isn't right. I'm the cause of your problems. My birthday is March fifteenth. I—"

His lips hovered just a breath from hers.

"You shouldn't be doing this," she told him.

"Probably not." He traced her bottom lip with his tongue. "But I heard your voice on March fifteenth when you called me, and I wanted you. I saw you sleeping on my couch and I wanted you. I want you right now." He nibbled kisses along her jawline. "I can't seem to help myself."

"I was going to betray you," she said. Somehow it seemed essential that she make that point clear. But her arms had moved of their own accord, and she was already threading her fingers through his hair, drawing that clever mouth to hers.

"You didn't," he said. "Why is that?"

"Because I want you." *I want you more than anything,* she thought.

"I want you, too," he murmured as he gathered her close and lifted her onto the bed.

MUCH LATER, she awoke and found herself alone in the bed. Moonlight, so bright it made her blink, poured through the sliding glass doors that formed one wall of the bedroom. Tony had left her. Climbing out of the bed, she drew on her sweats quickly and moved into the living room of the suite. There was no sign of him there, either.

Of course, he would leave her, she thought. She'd admitted that she wanted to betray him and his family. A man with strong loyalties like Tony Romano wouldn't risk betraying them. It wasn't until she stepped down into the sunken living room that she saw it.

He'd set up a small table for two in front of the fireplace. As her gaze drifted over the silver candelabra, the small bunch of lily-of-the-valley in a crystal vase, a lump formed in her throat. Before she'd told him her real reasons for coming here, he'd said he'd had something to show her.

Even as she blinked back a sting of tears, she moved

toward the table and picked up one stem of the lilies and inhaled its scent. Romance. It moved her that he'd wanted to give it to her.

The wave of regret struck her so solidly that she nearly took a step back. This was what she'd lost. For there wasn't a doubt in her mind that she'd lost Tony. Oh, he might give in to his desire for her. He was only human. But he wouldn't allow himself to feel anything more than that for her. He simply wouldn't be able to.

She moved to a nearby table and picked up a picture next to the one she'd studied when Lucy had first shown her into the apartment. The Romano men. The one she hadn't met must be Nick. Because she couldn't help herself, she ran one finger down Tony's image. He looked younger then—they all did. Sam was skinnier. After setting it down, she picked up the other framed photo on the table. She hadn't paid much attention to it earlier. She recognized A.J. in this one—and the woman standing next to Nick had to be his wife, Tyler Sheridan, the granddaughter of the woman Henry Romano had built this very suite for—Isabelle Sheridan. She glanced around the room. It was altogether too bad that they were going to lose the place that had bound them together for so long.

Then she had an idea, not quite sure what triggered it. Was it the name Sheridan? Was it the deep wave of longing that moved through her when she thought of the kind of family loyalty that the Romanos had always enjoyed? Or perhaps it was the fact that she'd moved toward the glass door that opened onto her patio and caught her reflection in the pane. The image of herself in the baggy sweats had stopped her in her tracks.

She looked exactly as she had two years ago. Oh, she

hadn't put on weight—at least not twenty-five pounds. It was the sweats that made her look heavier. But she was thinking like the old Lily also. She was slipping back into the old habit of not believing that she could have what she wanted.

She wanted to put a stop to whoever was threatening Tony.

She wanted to make sure that the Romano family could hold on to Henry's Place.

And she wanted Tony Romano.

A little voice in the back of her mind warned her that she was being greedy, that three goals were too much to hope for. Ignoring it, she headed for her cell phone because she had a pretty good idea how she could accomplish Goal 2. And if she was lucky, the other two might fall into her lap like dominos.

TONY PACED back and forth in his office. He hadn't been able to stay with Lily and not touch her again. She needed sleep and he needed to think. The small office he kept off the lobby was no larger than a monk's cell. It had been his father's office, too. If he stood, he could touch all the walls without moving. The first time he'd been able to do that, his father had smiled at him and told him he was a man. At times the small cubicle was the only place that allowed him the kind of isolation that was a very precious commodity in a hotel where family and guests demanded constant attention.

In front of him on his desk lay a small stack of index cards. On each of them, he'd printed a detail or event that had occurred since J. R. McNeil had first contacted him. While he'd been printing them out, he hadn't allowed himself to think about them or try to make connections. Now, he was going to deal the cards out on his desk in different arrangements and see what occurred. He'd never had the talent for investigative work that his brothers and his cousin Nick shared, but he'd often tried to figure out solutions to problems in the hotel using just this process.

From left to right he laid out the cards: McNeil Enterprises buys up block Henry's Place sits on; mechanical problems on the McNeil Enterprises jet; Lily's reservation canceled; Dame Vera predicts Tony Romano's luck is changing; Dame Vera predicts disaster—Ides of March is key; plumbing is sabotaged; Jerry Langford McNeil arrives, believing that Lily is still in Tahiti and he's taking over for her; Giles Fortescue arrives, motives multiple and questionable, claims he wants Henry's Place because of old rivalry; man in a blue car shoots at Tony or Lily or both of them; the blue sedan with the same shooter at the wheel tries to run them down.

Tony paused then and frowned as he recalled another blue car—the one he'd almost been hit by on his way home from that poker game with his brothers. What if that hadn't been an isolated incident? Quickly, he scribbled it on an index card and placed it next to the others. He'd take time later to brainstorm about how it might be related to the other facts. Right now he needed to get all the stuff out on the table.

He pondered the old rivalry between McNeil and Fortescue and his father's warning to never trust McNeil. After a moment of staring at the cards that now covered most of the surface of his desk, he grabbed another one and wrote: Lily returns to McNeil

Enterprises, determined to get father's long-denied approval and earn a vice presidency.

Tony frowned down at the letters he'd just printed. Did someone want to make sure that Lily didn't get the vice presidency? That would explain a lot of the facts detailed on the index cards. Drawing another out of the stack, he printed: Tony kisses Lily in the lobby of the hotel, letting everyone know that she most likely has an inside track to getting Henry's Place for McNeil.

But how did the attack on the plumbing fit in? And the attempted hit-and-run on him after the poker game at Sam's? Unless those were just unrelated incidents. Folding his hands behind his head, Tony let his mind sift through the possibilities, but he'd always had trouble with coincidences. With a sigh, he gathered up the cards, shuffled them and dealt them out on the desk again.

An hour later, he wasn't any closer to a definitive theory about who might be behind the attacks. But he was almost certain that the threat against Lily was real—a lot more real than his brothers believed. There was someone he needed to talk to about that. After consulting his Rolodex, he picked up his phone and dialed a number.

LILY FROWNED down at the papers she'd lined up in neat rows on the bed. Each one contained one part of the plan she'd come up with to save Henry's Place for the Romanos. It wasn't right yet, and for the life of her she couldn't figure out what was missing. From the time she'd been a little girl, it had helped her to write everything down and spread it out in columns or rows.

She often suspected she'd picked up the habit when

she'd spent long hours watching one of her nannies play solitaire. The experience had certainly given her a distaste of card games, but the neatness of the rows of papers, or perhaps the visual picture of her overall plan, usually stimulated her thought processes. The loans were the tricky part—better if they didn't come all from one place. She lifted that sheet and swapped it with the one marked "first-year expenditures." After studying the new configuration of problems and solutions, she was more convinced than ever that something was missing. Oh, she had enough to present at the meeting she'd arranged. But she'd have felt better if she had the whole solution.

When her cell phone rang, she welcomed the interruption. "Yes?"

"If you want to survive another twenty-four hours, leave Henry's Place right now."

"Who is this?" she asked. The voice had sounded tinny and mechanical. When there was no answer, she repeated the question. This time all that greeted her was a burst of static.

For a moment after she shut off her phone, Lily merely stared at it. For the first time, her anger outweighed her fear. If they thought they could scare her off, they had another think coming.

When her cell phone rang again, Lily pressed the button that would power it off. They were not going to frighten her.

It was only when the phone rang again that she realized it was the one on the table next to the bed.

She reached for it, then said, "Hello."

"I'll be picking you up in ten minutes," A.J. said. "Tyler's plane just left Boston. They'll be touching down on the runway at JFK in about thirty minutes. You've got your disguise?"

Lily glanced at the foot of the bed. "All I have to do is put it on." Lucy had provided her with a navy blazer, Grace with reading glasses and Alistair had sent up a fake mustache. Gina had come up with jeans and a man's hat. The latter had earned her speculative glances from her daughters. Hopefully, disguised as a man, Lily would be able to slip out of the hotel with no one the wiser.

"Are you ready for the meeting?" A.J. asked.

Lily glanced down at her columns of notes. "As ready as I'm going to get. How about you?" The plan she'd come up with required A.J.'s help. Tyler's too.

"All set. But there's a slight change in plans. Sam's coming with us."

Lily could hear what she thought was his voice, but she couldn't catch the words.

"He wouldn't let me come unless I agreed. But I really think he's afraid Tony will kill him if he lets you out of that hotel without his personal bodyguard services. But he agrees with me that the best place to have a family meeting that Tony can't interrupt is on Tyler's plane. Sam and I will be there shortly at the kitchen exit."

Lily glanced at her notes one last time, but there was no last-minute epiphany in her mind. She was going to have to go with what she had.

"WHEN I ASKED to borrow a costume, I didn't expect it to be a dress." Tony stared with more than a little dismay at his image in the mirror.

"Relax," Alistair said. "You only have to wear it until we get you safely into the limousine. Vera and I will have you back to your old self in plenty of time for your meeting with Mr. McNeil.''

Vera tugged the wig into place on his head. "Perfect.''

"I look like Miss Marple on a bad hair day,'' Tony said.

"Every day was a bad hair day for Jane Marple,'' Dame Vera said. "That's one of the reasons I always declined that role. The other was the appalling wardrobe. Jane Marple wasn't known for her fashion sense, either. There.'' She gave the wig a final pat. "You're good to go, as they say nowadays. All set, Alistair?''

"Always, my dear.'' After rising from his chair, he moved toward her and extended his arm.

"Just a minute.'' Vera reached into her bag and pulled out a pack of cigarettes, plucked one out and inserted it into a long silver holder. Then she placed her hand on Alistair's arm.

"I sincerely hope you are not going to smoke that, my dear.''

"Don't be silly. It's merely a prop. If Myrna Loy were alive, she'd be eating her heart out right now. I hope that the bar is stocked in the limousine.''

"You must have more faith in me than that, my dear. I ordered Leroy to chill the vodka and vermouth when I called to order the car brought round.''

"Well, I guess that's almost as good as champagne.''

"Shall we go?''

Tony followed in their wake as they swept out of the suite. All he'd wanted from his two favorite guests was a costume so that he could safely get by whatever men Drew and Sam had stationed outside the hotel. By the time they'd gotten him into the dress, Alistair and Vera had expanded his plan to include them and their limousine.

"You need a dresser to get you in and out of your costume," Alistair had explained.

"And you'll be safer this way," Dame Vera had assured him. "The limo is bulletproof. Alistair took care of that right after all those nasty political assassinations in the sixties."

Tony could only hope that the vehicle still ran. He had less than thirty minutes to get to the Plaza for the meeting he'd set up with J.R. and Pamela McNeil.

TYLER SHERIDAN ROMANO WAS was one of the most beautiful women Lily had ever seen. The blond hair and blue eyes, the classic features were just a part of it. Tyler had an inner glow that Lily suspected came from the family that surrounded her in the small office on her private jet. Nick Romano sat a short ways away with a sleeping baby tucked under one arm and a two-year-old boy with Tyler's blue eyes and his father's dark hair sitting beside him. At A.J.'s request, they'd detoured to JFK on their way to a business meeting in Atlanta.

A.J. stood, leaning over Tyler's shoulder, looking at the notes Lily had brought. Sam sat close by. He'd urged his wife to take a seat, but she'd claimed that the baby kicked less if she stood up. Lily found herself envying the closeness, the intimacy that seemed to flow so visibly between each couple.

"This is a marvelous plan," Tyler said, looking up from the papers to meet Lily's eyes. "I've been trying to convince Tony to let me pay for some of the renovations, but he wouldn't hear of it." She turned toward her husband and Sam. "The way Lily has structured it, we wouldn't be loaning Tony the money. Instead, each family member would be investing in the future of Henry's Place. In return, we'll each receive a certain number of ownership shares. Tony remains in charge—like any good CEO—but he'll have the money to make all the renovations that are needed."

"He may just go for it," Nick said. "His father asked him to keep the place afloat. It's been a matter of pride for him to keep that promise. But family is important to Tony. He's going to want to make sure that the hotel survives."

"And look at this," A.J. said, pointing to something on the paper in Tyler's hand. "Lily's proposing that we set up our investment in the hotel so that our profits go into a trust for our children and future Romanos. Tony can't accuse us of wanting to throw our money into a black hole with this clause as part of the package."

"He's always been so stubborn," Sam said.

"We're Romanos now. That means we're family," A.J. said, meeting her husband's eyes.

Tyler glanced over at Nick. "Yes, we are."

"You won't get any argument from me," Nick said.

"Me either," Sam said. "It's Tony we have to worry about."

Tyler looked back at Lily. "Once I explain this plan to him, he can't possibly think we'd be making a donation to a lost cause. Even with the improvements and renovations Lily has mapped out, the hotel should be turning a healthy profit in two years."

"I knew I liked her," A.J. said.

"I just have one question," Tyler said. "Why are you doing this?"

"Because I don't want Tony—I don't want any of you—to lose Henry's Place. I've only been there a couple of days, but I can see that it's more than a hotel to all of you. It's a home. It's where you gather to nurture each other, to draw strength from each other." She glanced at Sam. "I saw that today when you all came to the penthouse suite after the shooting."

"Okay. Then there's only one suggestion I have," Tyler said. "All the Romano women ought to be offered an opportunity to invest. For Grace and Lucy, it can be later when they have the money. But Gina should be invited now."

For the first time since she'd entered the small plane, Lily smiled. "Of course. I knew there was something missing, but I just couldn't put my finger on it."

"And you should invest too," Tyler said. "From what Sam and A.J. tell me, you'll be a Romano woman soon enough."

Lily felt her stomach sink. "No. Tony's not going to forget that I came here with the intention of stealing his hotel away from him. I just want to make sure he doesn't lose it."

Tyler set the papers down. "Well, the offer is open. You can change your mind. In the meantime, Nick and I did a little checking into why Tony's father might have warned him not to sell to McNeil."

"As far as I could see, McNeil and Henry Romano never met," Nick said. "There's no record of any business dealings."

"But it turns out that my grandmother had business as well as personal dealings with J. R. McNeil. She was engaged to him at one time. They'd even set the wedding date."

Lily stared at Tyler. "I never knew."

"You must have been a child. I certainly was. The only reason I came across the information is that my grandmother kept a series of journals and I'm trying to organize them into a biography. She met Henry the month before her wedding, and then she evidently changed her mind about the wedding."

"Did she say why?" Lily asked.

"She's not really clear on that one." Tyler smiled wryly. "My grandmother was a shrewd woman. I'm sure she kept the journals, knowing that the information would be made public after her death. She's vague about a lot of things."

"When was the wedding date?" Lily asked.

Tyler smiled. "Now that she *did* write down. They were to be married on March 15th."

"The Ides of March," Lily murmured. "Dame Vera said that everything started on the Ides of March."

9

TONY HADN'T BEEN IN one of the presidential suites at the Plaza before, and he was impressed as the hotel butler led him down a short hallway to a spacious sitting room. With a quick glance, he took in the plush cream-colored carpet dotted with what appeared to be authentic oriental rugs, fresh flowers on an ebony coffee table, and a wall of windows that in daylight would offer a view of Central Park. J. R. McNeil, looking warm and expansive, sat at a mahogany dining table. As the butler led him toward it, Tony studied the woman standing to his left. Pamela Langford-McNeil was a tall brunette in her early fifties, Tony guessed, but very well preserved. And she had the cold eyes of a shark.

"Would you like some coffee, Mr. Romano?" Pamela asked.

Tony glanced briefly at the silver urn on the nearby buffet, then shook his head. "No, thanks. I'd like to get down to business."

A flicker of annoyance passed over Pamela's carefully made-up features. "Jerry should really be in on this meeting. He'll be here shortly."

Impatience flashed into J.R.'s eyes. "You can fill Jerry in later, Pamela. Obviously, what Mr. Romano has come to say is urgent. Otherwise, he would not have requested this meeting at such a late hour."

Tony studied the man seated across from him at the table. He was in his late sixties. That much he knew from the background check that Sam had run. His first wife, Lily's mother, had died shortly after Lily was born. He'd married Pamela Langford when Lily was ten. J.R. carried the years well, and from the neatly styled hair right down to the personally tailored suit, he looked every bit the successful CEO of a multi-million-dollar corporation. But for the life of him, Tony couldn't picture the man as Lily's father. Perhaps because the warmth that the man exuded was merely a mask.

J.R.'s lips curved in a smile that didn't reach his cool gray eyes. "I'd like to apologize for my daughter's ineptness in representing McNeil."

Beneath the table, Tony's hands clenched into fists. "She isn't inept."

"Inexperienced, then," Pamela said. "You'll be much more comfortable dealing with Jerry. He's had lots of—"

"I won't be dealing with Jerry." Tony kept his eyes on McNeil's. "The only person from McNeil Enterprises that I intend to deal with is Lily. In fact, I called this meeting in part to let you know that you've made the trip to New York for nothing."

J.R.'s eyes narrowed. "And what was the other part of your reason for requesting this meeting?"

"I don't want you to show up at Henry's Place unless you're invited because I don't want Lily upset."

J.R. leaned back in his chair. "So that's the way it is."

"That's the way it is." Neither of the two people facing him looked happy.

"That's it? That's what you came out here to say?" J.R. finally asked.

"No." Tony leaned back in his chair. "I want to know the real reason why you offered to buy Henry's Place last month."

"I told you—"

"You told me squat." Tony leaned forward. "You've bought up the entire block surrounding the hotel."

"I don't know what you're talking about," J.R. said.

Tony waved a hand. "Don't bother lying. My brother and my cousin have checked it out. Giles Fortescue is ready to participate in a bidding war for the hotel. And someone is trying very hard to put Lily or me or both of us out of the picture. In the past twenty-four-hours we've been shot at and nearly run down."

Tony could have sworn that J.R.'s skin whitened beneath his tan. "If you're accusing me—"

Tony raised a hand. "No. I'm not accusing you. I wanted you to know that this 'deal' you're involved in has put your daughter's life at risk. And I'm warning you—if you're behind the attacks, I'll find out and I'll expose you."

"Now wait just a minute." Some of the color had returned to J.R.'s face. "I would never do anything to harm my daughter. And I don't make a habit of killing people just so that I can buy their hotels."

J.R. had made a smooth recovery, Tony thought, but something that he'd said to the older man had shaken the him. If he could just pinpoint exactly what it was... In an attempt to penetrate McNeil's very smooth facade again, he asked, "Why did my father tell me never to sell to you?"

Surprise flickered in his eyes before the shutters

slipped back into place. Everything else aside, Tony realized that he might actually enjoy playing poker with Lily's father.

"He told you that?" J.R. asked.

Tony recognized the question as an attempt to stall. The older man was trying to gather his thoughts. "What did you do to him to make him distrust you that much?"

J.R. drew the pen through his fingers again. "Nothing. Your father was the man who couldn't be trusted. He stole away a woman I was about to marry."

This time it was Tony's turn to be surprised. He glanced at Pamela and he would have bet that this was news to her also.

"Who?" And then the answer came to him as suddenly and definitively as little lottery balls slipping into slots. "Isabelle Sheridan. You're after my hotel because of something that happened over twenty years ago?"

"No." J.R. was in control again. "My offer to buy your hotel is strictly business."

There was something that J.R. wasn't telling him. Tony was sure of it. But he was out of ammunition and time.

J.R. rose from the table and extended his hand. "I'm looking forward to hearing my daughter's report, Mr. Romano. And don't worry, I won't visit the hotel without an invitation."

LILY CLOSED THE DOOR of the penthouse suite and leaned back against it. The first hint of dawn was graying the sky, but the room was dark—darker than it had been earlier with the moonlight streaming through the glass. She knew that the place was empty. If Tony had returned while she was away, he would have called Sam the moment he discovered she was missing. Barring that, he would have been waiting for her, ready to pounce as soon as she came in.

Pressing the heel of her hand against the tightening sensation in her chest, she told herself that it was relief she should be feeling. If he'd been here waiting, there would have been hell to pay. If he'd been here waiting, she would have been willing to pay it. If he'd just been here.

She moved down to the table that he'd set for her earlier in front of the fireplace. She missed him. It had been only a few hours since he'd been here, since they'd made love, and she missed him. Picking up the vase filled with lily-of-the-valley, she inhaled their scent and wondered how much she was going to miss Tony Romano when he was out of her life for good.

A sound had her turning and moving toward the window. She knew that Sam had a man stationed on the roof somewhere, but this would have been the first time that she'd heard him. For a moment the footsteps paused, and she concentrated on identifying the shadows that she could see. The darker shapes about ten yards away had to be the potted trees that separated the penthouse patio from the rest of the roof.

The footsteps began again, and it was only a moment before a shadow separated itself from the row of trees and began to move slowly toward the door. Straining her eyes, she tried to see who it was. But the light was too dim. She could have sworn that whoever it was wore a cloak of some sort that swung about his feet as he moved. The sound of the footsteps was muffled, almost as if the person was tiptoeing.

Could it be Tony? But surely, Tony wouldn't be in a cloak. Nor would he be sneaking so stealthily across the patio. Operating under the principle that it was better to be safe than sorry, she grabbed the candelabra off the table and hurried to hide behind the door to the suite.

The knob began to turn slowly just as she flattened her back against the wall. Raising the candelabra above her head, she braced herself and waited. For ten long seconds—she counted every one—nothing happened. Any remaining hope she had that this was Tony drained away. Surely, Tony would have walked right in.

A scenario began to build itself in her mind as fear fed her imagination. The shooter had somehow gained access to the hotel. The bald man in the sunglasses had eliminated the man stationed on the roof. And now he was ready to eliminate Tony.

Still the door didn't open.

Had the intruder heard her? Was he waiting and listening just as she was? Only because she had to, Lily drew in a quiet breath and let it out. Her arms were beginning to complain loudly when the door finally began to open. Stepping out of its way, she swung her arms down.

There was the sound of a thud, then someone swore loudly. She had time to absorb that much before she was shoved so hard into the wall that she dropped the candelabra. The impact was still singing through her when her arms were grabbed and pinned above her head. She opened her mouth to scream, but a hand clamped over it.

"Lily?"

She recognized the voice at once, even though he spoke in a whisper. Tony. Relief streamed through her.

"Is that you?"

She tried to nod against the hand that covered her mouth.

"Is there anyone else in the suite?"

This time she gave her head a negative shake.

Immediately, he released her and whispered, "What the hell is going on? What have you got on your mouth?"

For the first time, Lily remembered that she was still in disguise. How was she going to explain that? She didn't want him to know about her meeting with Tyler and A.J. Not yet. Before she could answer, Tony reached behind her and flipped on the lights. Then he simply stared at her.

"It's a mustache," he said. "You're wearing a mustache."

She lifted her chin as she looked him over with the same interest that he was bestowing on her. "You're wearing a dress. And a wig."

He tore the wig off and tossed it on the couch. "I had to wear a disguise to get out of the hotel safely." Then his eyes narrowed and the heat in them nearly seared her right to the bone. "That's what you're trying to do, isn't it?" Then gripping her arms, he gave her a shake. "Admit it. You're trying to sneak out of here in that get-up, aren't you?"

If that was the conclusion he wanted to jump to, Lily

was only too happy to encourage the leap. Better that than have to admit that she'd already done it.

"Can't you get it through your head that someone may be trying to kill you?" He gave her another shake.

"Or you." She twisted herself free enough to poke him in the chest. "It's okay for you to go parading off around the city wearing a dress, but I have to stay cooped up here?"

"Yes!" he shouted.

"In a pig's eye," she shouted back.

"You two okay?"

The voice from the doorway had them both spinning toward it. Lily recognized him as the man who'd escorted her down to Sam and A.J.'s waiting car. Something in the way they both looked at him had him raising his hands palms out. "Just checking. Sam will have my head if anything...well...I can see that I'm..." He paused and made a choking sound. "I can see that...I'm interrupting—" He broke off as the laugh escaped, a deep-throated sound. "Sorry." One hand on his stomach, the other still raised, he backed off a step. "I heard...the shouting." This time the laugh came right up from his belly.

Picking up his skirt so he wouldn't trip, Tony strode to the door. "Say one word about this to my brother, and you will regret it."

"Right...I understand." The rest of his laughter was muffled as Tony slammed the door.

When Tony turned back to her, he looked embarrassed, frustrated, and furious. His hair was sticking up in all directions, and he had the skirt of a flowered dress fisted in his hand. Her stomach plummeted and she felt herself take a quick hard tumble into love.

Had she just fallen in love with a man who looked mad enough to shake her? Panic warred with laughter—but laughter won, and she couldn't prevent it from escaping.

She coughed, trying to disguise it. "You're wearing a dress. I'm wearing a mustache." Helpless, she didn't bother with the cough when another laugh slipped out. "Can you imagine what he thought?"

Tony glared at her. "Several scenarios come to mind and I'm not interested in any of them getting out on the street or back to my family." He paused for a moment, his eyes narrowing. "You think this is funny."

The amazement in his voice had her doubling over. Drawing in a deep breath, she gasped, "Hilarious." Then as the next laugh escaped, she sank to the floor. "That dress gives new meaning to the phrase fashion emergency. You should see yourself."

"I did, and it's not an experience I care to repeat. How about you? Looked in the mirror lately?"

She glanced up then, swiped at her eyes. "What?"

"Your mustache is crooked." His temper hadn't run its course, but watching her doubled over with mirth, he felt it draining. In a second he was crouched down on the floor in front of her. "Here, let me fix it." He yanked it off.

Startled, she pressed her fingers to her upper lip, then he watched her eyes fill with laughter again. This time he joined her. As the sound of his laughter filled the air, he began to feel relaxed for the first time since the car had nearly run them down.

By the time they'd regained some control, he was sitting beside her on the floor, his arm around her shoulders. He decided against asking her where she'd intended to go in her disguise. If she told him, he'd probably just become angry again. Instead, he asked, "Where did you get the mustache?"

"Alistair," she said.

He grinned. "Figures. Dame Vera was kind enough to lend me the dress and the wig. I'm betting she wouldn't be caught dead in either one." He patted her knee with his hand. "You'll be happy to know that I took them off before I talked with your father."

She twisted on the floor so that she could face him. "You met with my father?"

He nodded, then tightened his grip on her shoulder when she started to say something. "We didn't talk business. I told him that the only McNeil I would do any business with was you."

"But...then, I don't understand. Why did you go to see him?"

He took her chin in his hands so that she had to meet his eyes. "He's your father. He has a right to know that someone is trying to hurt you." He couldn't say kill. He didn't want to dwell on the fact that he could have lost her twice in one day. He needed to keep his mind clear if he was ever going to figure out what was going on.

When her eyes widened, he said, "What?"

"I just remembered. I got a phone call—on my cell phone a couple of hours ago. The voice was disguised, but whoever it was warned me that I'd be sorry if I didn't clear out of this hotel."

"What were the exact words?"

"If you want to survive another twenty-four hours, leave Henry's Place right now."

"Then perhaps you *were* the intended victim of the shooter." He ran his hands through his hair. "I've got a

whole list of people who would benefit from you being
out of the picture. What if your father's company plane
was purposely tampered with to keep you in Tahiti
and away from Henry's Place? Who would have
stepped up to the plate for you?"

"Jerry."

"And he's not the only one on my list. If something
happened to you right now, what do you think would
be the chances of my selling to McNeil? And who
might I turn to?"

"Giles," Lily said frowning.

"Exactly."

"But that car wasn't particular about who it was running down."

Tony shrugged. "I had told him I wasn't interested
in selling. If he got rid of me in the bargain, that would
pretty much ensure the sale of the hotel. Then Giles
and Jerry duke it out, and my money's on Giles."

"He couldn't be sure your family would sell to Fortescue Investments," Lily pointed out.

"He'd rely on his negotiating skills for that."

Lily thought for a minute. "I could see that...."

He turned to study her. "You just can't picture him
as a killer. Does he still mean that much to you?"

She sighed. "No. The only thing I feel when I think of
Giles is that I was stupid to fall for his line. But when I
think of him as a killer—I tried when I was sitting
across from him at the Waldorf—my gut feeling is that
the man doesn't have the passion for murder."

"He doesn't have to. He can hire someone to do it,"
Tony said flatly. "And if he gets rid of you and Henry's
Place becomes his, he also has his revenge on McNeil

for the fiasco of your broken engagement two years ago."

"So?" She slipped her fingers through his. "How do we stop him?"

He looked into her eyes and wished he knew the answer. "I don't know. Sam and Drew are working overtime to come up with something." Pulling her close, he then kissed her nose and drew her to her feet. "C'mon. I'm going to sleep on it. Something will occur to me."

She shot him a look as he led her into the bedroom. "We never just sleep in that bed."

"This time we will." He traced one finger over the dark circles under her eyes. "I'm not attracted to women with mustaches."

"I'm not wearing it anymore." Then she burst into laughter as he scooped her up, carried her into the bedroom and fell with her onto the bed.

THE LIVING ROOM of the suite was once more filled with Romanos. And they were eating again. Lily shook her head in amazement at the trays that Gina and Lucy were passing. As usual everyone was talking at once. Frustration and fear were fueling tempers. Drew had gotten a positive ID on the man who'd shot at them and nearly run them down, but so far, he hadn't been picked up. Sam had struck pay dirt with a contact at the mayor's office who had a seat on the city planning commission. There were rumors that a new luxury hotel and conference center in the theater district was about to be placed on their meeting agenda. So there was a lot riding on McNeil Enterprises getting hold of Henry's Place.

They still had nothing concrete, but Giles Fortescue

had risen to the top of the suspect list. The question fueling the current debate was how to trap him.

The Romanos were shouting ideas at one another. Nick and Sam were hunched over Sam's laptop, Drew was pacing, and Tony sat on one of the love seats listening to and discarding ideas.

The only other person in the room not yelling out her opinion was Tyler Sheridan who was sitting on the couch next to Lily. Even A.J. was pounding her fist on the table to argue about something Nick had said.

"It's the Mediterranean temperament," Tyler said, leaning close and pitching her voice so that Lily could hear her. "They'll run out of steam sooner or later, and then's a good time to pitch your own idea."

She would if she had one. She glanced at the kitchen area where Alistair was lounging against the counter sipping coffee. Dame Vera sat next to him on a stool, waving her silver cigarette holder to emphasize something she was saying. They were dressed in their *Thin Man* costumes, and they were the embodiment of all the late-night TV mysteries she'd ever seen.

It was then that the germ of an idea struck her. And by the time the chaotic discussion in front of her had mellowed somewhat, she was ready to share it.

10

TONY DIDN'T LIKE the plan Lily had come up with the day before one bit. But he'd been outvoted. Gripping the iron railing that bordered the patio garden, he stared out at the city. Nerves had tied oily knots in his stomach. The men had been banished to the patio by the Romano women so that if they got into a fight, they wouldn't ruin the setting for the little play that they were about to enact.

Drawing in a deep breath, he looked out at the rows and rows of buildings—spires of steel and concrete, reaching for the sky. Usually, the city calmed him in a way that he imagined a sailor was soothed when he looked out over the sea.

But not tonight, not while he was replaying the little charade Lily had cooked up to trap whoever was behind the shootings. She'd called it a fitting April Fools' joke. He didn't think it was funny.

It didn't matter how good her idea was or how much sense it made. The bottom line was that she'd come up with a plan that might trap the one man she'd spent her whole life trying to please—her father. He didn't think J. R. McNeil was behind the attempts on his life and Lily's. *His* favorite candidate was Giles Fortescue. Still, he wasn't sure. And he didn't like that Lily had been put in this very awkward position. But like it or not, in the end, his family had used logic to argue away every objection he made. Logic was something he'd always prided himself on, but he couldn't seem to summon any up where Lily was concerned.

So they were throwing an impromptu engagement party.

Giles Fortescue along with J.R., Pamela, and Jerry McNeil, had been invited to the penthouse suite at Henry's Place to celebrate Lily and Tony's engagement. Not that the engagement had been Lily's idea. No, that little detail had been added by his family as they discussed, debated and fought over the trap that they were going to set.

"Make it an engagement party," Nick had said. "If you're going to set a trap, make sure it has teeth."

One by one, everyone had agreed. But Lily had not looked happy about it. That only added a twist to the knot in his stomach.

"An engagement announcement is bound to push somebody's buttons," A.J. had said.

That was the comment that had stuck in Tony's mind. Whoever's buttons they pushed might decide to take action against Lily.

If he could have been objective about it—the way his brothers and cousins could—Tony would have described the plan that Lily had come up with as brilliant. But he'd lost all objectivity where Lily was concerned. If she'd broached her idea to him privately, he would have nipped it in the bud. But she'd sprung it in front of his family, and after that it had taken on a life of its own.

Even Drew had been enough in favor of the plan to get a judge to sign off the recording devices they were going to use, and Sam had wired the entire suite. Tony glanced at his watch. In less than thirty minutes, Giles Fortescue, J.R., Pamela, and Jerry McNeil would arrive for cocktails. The curtain would go up.

He turned just as Nick joined him at the railing.

"This is the quickest way to catch the bastard," Nick said.

Drew was pacing, talking into his cell phone. Sam was focused on his laptop, Alistair was looking over his shoulder. They were working, but the answers weren't coming quickly enough.

Tony sighed. "I know. It's only on TV and in the movies that the police and P.I.s solve cases in sixty minutes. But what if Lily's little charade doesn't work?"

Nick nodded toward Sam and Drew. "Then we'll let the cop and the P.I. solve it, and you can lock Lily up for however long it takes."

"Shit," Drew said into his cell phone.

"Dammit," Sam said in disgust, shaking his head at his laptop.

"The happy sounds of progress," Nick said, patting Tony on the back. Then he added, "Too bad we're too dressed up to play a little hoop. That would take the edge off."

"I could beat you even wearing a monkey suit," Sam said, closing his laptop.

Nick laughed. "Not a chance. I know your tricks."

Drew pocketed his cell phone and looked at his cousin. "Care to put your money where your mouth is?"

"Absolutely not," Alistair said. It had been at his insistence that the Romano men all wore tuxedos. "Do you want to meet with Fortescue and the McNeils looking like a bunch of hooligans? The whole purpose behind the tuxedos is to intimidate your guests. Do you want to lose your edge?"

"He's right," Tony said. "We have to hold it together until this whole thing is over." That was what he'd been telling himself all day.

"What you're all experiencing is stage fright," Alistair said. "A little deep breathing will alleviate the problem, and there will be no wear and tear on the costumes. Balanchine created this routine for the American Ballet Company. Now just bend over at the waist and let your arms flop." Alistair demonstrated. "Shake out your wrists."

There was a definite plea in the glances Tony's family shot him. Drew, the closest one to Tony, muttered under his breath. "Ballet? I agreed to the monkey suit, but—"

Tony bit back a grin and said, "We'll behave, Alistair. But what would settle my nerves even more than deep-breathing exercises would be to run over the plan one more time."

His brothers were more than happy to oblige him.

"I'm always nervous before a performance," Dame Vera said.

Lily stared into the full-length mirror as the older woman dabbed color onto her cheeks. The other women had exited the room only a few minutes before, claiming that they had to get into their costumes. Lucy, Dame Vera and Alistair were in charge of serving food and drinks. Gina and Grace were assigned to the kitchen. The rest were supposed to mingle with the guests—just as she was supposed to do until it was time to give the performance of her life.

"Now just remember, let all your muscles go lax and sink to the floor—just like we rehearsed," Vera said. "Watch." Stabbing a hand into her stomach, Vera groaned, then crumpled onto the floor. After a moment, she opened one eye. "I did this for two hundred and sixty straight performances of *Romeo and Juliet* at the Old Vic."

"That's the point. You've had practice. This will be my debut performance," Lily said.

"You know what they say. Dying's easy. Comedy's hard. You'll be fine." Dame Vera got to her feet. Lily had to admire the flexibility the older woman had. In the trim black pants and white jacket that she was wearing to tend bar, Dame Vera looked younger than she had when Lily had first met her in the lobby of the hotel. That day she'd reminded Lily of a witch, a tired one. But tonight, there was…something in her eyes. Of course, Vera had tied her long white hair into a neat bun, and that made a difference. But it was more than that. She looked less remote, more…

"The costume should help, too," Vera said, backing off so that she could study it. "Gina outdid herself."

Lily couldn't have agreed more. The dress was a deep royal blue that fell from thin straps on her shoulders to just above her knees. A Gina original would give any woman's confidence a boost.

And Lily needed it the next moment when Tony walked into the room. For a space of time she couldn't say a word. All she could do was stare at the image next to hers in the full-length mirror. He was a hand-

some man, charming, but in a tuxedo, he looked ruth-
less and invincible.

"Bond," he said finally, breaking the spell. "James
Bond."

She smiled then and turned to face him. "I've always
wanted to be a Bond girl."

"Well," Dame Vera said as she looked from one to
the other and backed toward the door, "I'll just leave
you two alone for a minute. But don't take too long.
Curtain is in ten minutes."

For a moment after the door to the bedroom shut,
neither of them said anything. Nerves. She could see
them in his eyes, hear them hum above the silence
stretching between them.

"It's going to be all right," she said, taking a quick
step towards him. "Your family has thought of everything, I think."

"Except for this." He reached into his pocket. "An
engagement needs a ring."

She was afraid to look at it, so she stalled until he'd
taken her hand and slipped it on her finger. Then he
lifted her hand and kissed it. "It was my mother's. And
it fits you just right. I'm going to take that as a good-
luck omen, Goldilocks."

She did look at it then—a diamond flanked by two
emeralds. Her chest constricted. The engagement
wasn't real, she reminded herself. It couldn't be real.

There was a knock on the door and Dame Vera
poked her head in. "Alistair says five minutes to curtain. We have to take our places."

Tony kept his eyes on Lily's. "When this is over—"

"Sorry," Nick said as he joined Dame Vera in the
doorway. "Drew has something he wants you to see."

With a sigh, Tony released Lily's hand and exited with his brother. Dame Vera hurried forward and took Lily's hand. "Perfect."

But it wasn't perfect, Lily thought. The diamond ring made her hope for something that couldn't be.

"It isn't the little charade we're staging that has you so worried, is it?" Vera asked.

Lily had to smile. "Have you always had this talent for reading minds?"

Dame Vera laughed. "I'm an actress. I've had to learn over the years to observe people very closely, to guess what they're thinking, what makes them tick. But I wouldn't need any special talent or even my crystal to see that you've fallen in love with Tony."

Lily sighed. "It's that obvious?"

Laughing again, Vera slipped an arm around her waist. "I'm psychic, remember?"

"I wish I knew what to do," Lily said.

"Deception clouds your thinking—especially self-deception. You just have to clarify what you want and go after it. That's what I'm doing with Alistair. I never married, never moved in with a man, because I always wanted to be independent. Thanks to the sabotaged plumbing, I've decided that I rather like living with Alistair. And I intend to take him up on the many offers of marriage he's made me over the past twenty years. Only," she paused to laugh again, "he doesn't know that yet."

Lily couldn't prevent a smile. "When will you let him know?"

"I'm going to break it to him gently. I'm sure it will come as a shock, and he's not as young as he used to be." She paused to take Lily's hand and study the ring. "And he never put an engagement ring on my finger."

"It's a fake. I mean, the engagement's a sham—it's just part of the whole charade we're playing tonight." Just looking at the diamond and emeralds had her stomach clenching. "I wish you could look into your crystal ball and tell me that Tony is going to be safe."

Dame Vera squeezed Lily's hand. "I wish I could, too. But the danger isn't over yet. That's why we're enacting this scene tonight."

"I'm just not as sure as Tony is that the villain is Giles."

Dame Vera's pencil-thin brows shot up. "Why not?"

"Because when I cast Giles as the man behind everything—I can't make all the puzzle pieces fit together."

"Which ones don't fit?" Vera asked.

"Your prediction about the Ides of March for one. You said the coming disaster was connected to the Ides of March." As she stood there trying to put the thoughts tumbling around in her head into words, Lily pictured the scene vividly in her mind. When Dame Vera had first said the words, lightning had flashed and thunder had rattled the glass doors of the hotel. "For a long time, I thought that I was going to trigger some disaster because my birthday is the fifteenth of March and I was lying about why I'd really come to Henry's Place. Today we learned that my father was once engaged to Isabelle Sheridan and they were supposed to be married on the fifteenth of March. If Tony's father was involved in the breakup, then my father could be out for revenge. But surely, he wouldn't want to kill me."

Vera took Lily's hands in hers. "This is very difficult for you."

"Tony's sure that Giles is behind everything. But he doesn't have any connection to the Ides of March."

"Not that we know of."

"True." Lily let out a breath on a sigh. Even as she did, something flickered at the edges of her mind, then faded away.

Dame Vera slipped her arm around Lily's waist and stood with her facing the mirror. "Well, we'll know the truth soon enough. In the *Thin Man* movies Myrna Loy and William Powell were always most confused just before they solved the mystery. And that's what's going to happen tonight."

"I hope you're right."

"The great thing about acting is that when you throw yourself into the role and step out on that stage, you just have to concentrate on playing the part. The world and its worries just fade away. A play is much simpler than real life."

Lily couldn't have agreed more.

TONY GLANCED AROUND the penthouse suite. Thanks to Alistair and Dame Vera, the set was perfect. Candlelight flickered, silver champagne buckets gleamed, and string quartet music drifted out of speakers. Drew was in the living room. He was wired so that he could keep in contact with the men monitoring the electronic surveillance equipment that Sam had installed. Sam and Nick were still on the patio with their wives. They would stay there until the guests started to arrive. Dame Vera was at her station behind the bar ready to take drink orders. Gina, Grace and Lucy were in the kitchen seeing to the hors d'ouevres. The only person missing was Lily.

Just as he was about to move across the room and knock on the bedroom door, it opened and she stepped into the room. Even though he'd already seen her for that brief moment in the bedroom, Tony felt his mind go blank. He'd thought her beautiful whenever the light struck her in a certain way, but right now she was stunning.

"She looks like a Hitchcock heroine," Alistair said in a low tone. "Grace Kelly in *Dial M for Murder*."

As long as it wasn't Janet Leigh in *Psycho*, Tony thought.

The doorbell rang and he pushed the thought out of his mind. He needed a clear head to play his part.

Giles was the first arrival, and Alistair greeted him at the door. Fortescue had brought a rose and a box of chocolates. Smiling, Lily moved to take both out of his hands. In spite of the fact that Lily had promised Giles was as predictable as snow in December, Tony breathed a sigh of relief. They could have staged the scene without the chocolates, but it would have been trickier. He hoped the candy was an omen that the rest of the evening would run smoothly.

"YOU'RE BREATHTAKING in that dress," Giles said.

Smiling, Lily decided to follow Dame Vera's advice and throw herself into the role. "I'm glad you came. I was hoping that you would forgive me for yesterday. I was...upset."

His eyebrows shot up. "Indeed, you were. I thought for a minute you were going to upend the contents of that vase on my head. The Lily I remember was shy and very mild-mannered."

A smile tugged at her lips. "I've changed."

He let his gaze roam over her. "Indeed you have."

"Let's drink to that." Lily led the way to the bar and waited while Dame Vera filled two flutes with champagne. She set down the rose and then opened the box of chocolates before placing it on the bar and reaching for her champagne.

Giles took her hand and examined the ring. "I'd offer my congratulations, but I'm worried about you."

"Why?"

"Romano works fast. Hasn't it occurred to you that this whirlwind courtship might be connected to the fact that he feels you're his ticket to hanging on to his hotel?"

Because she wasn't sure how to reply, she opted for saying nothing.

Giles squeezed her hand again before he released it. "I have a solution to your dilemma. Encourage your Mr. Romano to sell out to me, and you can be sure he's marrying you for yourself."

Leave it to Giles to figure a way to play all the angles. Lily couldn't help but admire him for it. "Are you going to tell me why you're really so anxious to get hold of this place?"

The look on his face was all innocence. "But I have." He touched his flute to hers. "Here's to your future happiness."

The doorbell rang again just as Tony entered through the patio doors. When Giles turned toward him, she put a hand on his arm. "One question. What do you think of when I say the Ides of March?"

She could have sworn that the puzzlement on his face was genuine.

"Shakespeare's *Julius Caesar*. Takes me back to tenth grade when I had to memorize Marc Antony's funeral speech."

"Anything else?"

"Wait. Yes, March fifteenth is also your birthday, right? What is this about?"

She could hear her father's and stepmother's voices behind her "Just a little bet I'm having with myself." Then turning, she moved toward her family. Giles was innocent. She felt it in her gut. Just as she now felt that one of the three people approaching her was guilty. But why would one of them resort to murder?

"GILES FORTESCUE," Giles said, extending his hand as Tony stepped toward him. "I don't believe we've been formally introduced."

Tony shook his hand.

"Congratulations. I wish you more success than I had in keeping her."

For just a moment, Tony studied the man standing in front of him. *Smooth* was the first word that came to mind. But sharks were smooth customers, too. *Soft* was the second word—a soft handshake, soft voice, and in spite of the fact that he was paying a tailor a fortune to disguise it, he was getting soft in the middle. Giles Fortescue wasn't a man who would do well in a dark alley. But the eyes were intelligent. He might very well be a man who would know how to hire people to do his dirty work. "Thank you. I don't intend to let her go."

And he didn't. Impatience streamed through him. He wanted the charade to be over. Beyond Giles's shoulder, he saw Pamela Langford-McNeil air-kiss the space near Lily's cheek. He wanted to go to Lily right now and take her someplace where they could talk and settle things between them. He was in love with her. It was a hell of a time to realize it. And he still wasn't sure when it had happened. All he knew was that he wanted the ring on her finger to symbolize a real engagement.

Shoving his impatience down, he shifted his gaze to Giles and said, "Why are you so anxious to buy this hotel?"

Giles laughed. "I've explained my motivations at length to Lily. McNeil wants this hotel. Ergo, I want it. It's really quite that simple. Adolescent but simple."

Perhaps, Tony thought. But the man standing in front of him appeared too suave and experienced to engage in an adolescent rivalry unless there was a significant advantage to be gained. Would he commit murder to gain that advantage? Lily thought not. Tony wasn't so sure.

"WHAT THE HELL IS GOING ON?" J.R. spoke the words in a hushed tone as he pulled Lily close and wrapped his arms around her.

Lily couldn't recall the last time her father had hugged her. Had he ever? "We're celebrating my engagement."

When J.R. released her, she tried to read his expression. But he was already scanning the room.

"Romano told me that someone had taken a shot at you and then tried to run you down."

Was it concern she heard in his voice? "Two near misses."

"Dammit. Fortescue really wants this hotel. He might be crazy enough to try to get you out of the way. I want you to tell Romano that you're stepping out of it. Convince him that you'll be safer if he deals directly with me." He squeezed her shoulders. "Pamela and I knew that this job might be a bit too much for you to handle. It's time for Daddy to come to the rescue."

Lily felt her stomach sink. He wasn't worried about her. He wasn't even happy that she'd gotten engaged. The only thing he was worried about was that she wouldn't be able to get him Henry's Place. A kaleidoscope of memories flooded her mind—other moments when her father had doubted her. Always before, the hurt had destroyed her. But this time all she felt was anger. Lily straightened her shoulders and managed a smile. "You worry too much, Daddy. I have everything under control."

"And turn your cell phone on. We agreed that you would keep it on at all times so that I could closely supervise what you're doing. I haven't been able to reach you all day."

Something clicked in the back of her mind. She'd turned her cell phone off right after that threatening message she'd received. And something had been niggling at her ever since. Only her father was supposed to have the number. She took his arm and steered him toward the bar. "By the way, I received a threatening call on my cell phone last night. Do you know who has the number besides you?"

He frowned impatiently. "No one."

"Did you write it down anywhere?"

"Just on the Rolodex in my office."

That meant Jerry, Pamela, and Olivia Bates, her fa-

ther's executive assistant, had access. She waited until
J.R. had waved away champagne and ordered a Scotch
before she said, "The person who called me this morning on my cell disguised his or her voice, and threatened to kill me. Giles may not be the only person who's
anxious to get me out of the way."

J.R. turned to stare at her for a moment. "You surely
can't believe that I had anything to do with it."

Drawing in a deep breath, Lily asked, "Did you?"

Her father stared at her for a second. Then he
frowned and made a dismissive gesture with his hand.
"You're being ridiculous."

"What about Pamela or Jerry?"

J.R.'s eyes narrowed then. "You're not thinking
clearly. I wouldn't put it past Fortescue to have a spy in
my office. He'd sink to any depths. Look at him."

Lily did just that. Giles was across the room, sipping
champagne and talking to Tony. Jerry had bypassed
the bar and was headed toward them with the speed of
a billiard ball straight out of a break.

Her father's point was a good one. Giles might have
been clever enough to get hold of her cell number. But
the fact remained—Jerry and Pamela wouldn't have
had to break a sweat to get it.

Right on cue, A.J. and Sam moved toward the bar.
Lily introduced her father to them and then made her
way to Pamela.

"ROMANO."

Tony turned to see Jerry McNeil approaching.

"I'm sorry I missed your meeting with J.R. and my
mother."

The news of the meeting, which Tony guessed was

intended to ruffle Giles, failed to do so. Jerry lacked Giles's sophistication and also his talent for keeping his feelings buried. Right now, there was anger in Jerry's eyes, barely suppressed. The same anger had been in his eyes yesterday morning in the hotel lobby. Tony wondered who it was aimed at. Giles? Or Lily? In his rush to cross the room Jerry had completely ignored his stepsister. Now he was ignoring Giles.

"If I might have a word with you?" Jerry asked.

No, Jerry Langford-McNeil didn't have the polish or the subtlety of Giles Fortescue. And he would offer no challenge in a poker game.

"If you can make it short," Tony said.

"Two minutes," Jerry promised. "If we could go someplace private?"

"Don't mind me. I'll just take a look at the view," Giles said amiably as he turned and strolled away.

Tony glanced over to see Lily talking to Pamela. A.J. and Sam had drawn J.R. out onto the patio. The box of chocolates was still open on the bar. Soon, everyone would be in place.

PAMELA LANGFORD-McNEIL TURNED from watching her son as Lily drew near. The older woman looked stunning as usual in a short black cocktail suit. Her hair was pulled back into a twist at the back of her neck, and diamonds glittered in her ears. The smile she gave Lily didn't reach her eyes. "You've made a rare mess of things, as usual."

Lily's chin lifted. "Here I was thinking that I was handling everything quite well."

Pamela spoke in a low tone that held a hint of malice. "Your father doesn't think so. I warned him not to send you. The company is still recovering from the hit the stocks took when you broke off your engagement with Giles. Jerry would have had this deal sewn up by now. The least you can do is let him handle it from now on."

Lily studied her for a minute. "Is that why you made sure that the company plane had major mechanical problems in Tahiti? So that Jerry could take my place?"

Something flickered in Pamela's eyes. "You've definitely gone off the deep end this time. Now you have a persecution complex."

"Someone threatened my life this morning. And they used a cell phone that only a handful of people could access. You and Jerry are two of those people. Only you forgot something. There are records. Wireless calls can be traced."

Lily had the satisfaction of seeing pure hatred contort Pamela's features for one full second before the woman managed to get control. Then Lily smiled and walked away.

JERRY TOOK A SIP from the glass of champagne Vera had handed him. Then he drew Tony a few steps away from the bar. "Lily is lying to you," he said in a low tone.

Tony narrowed his eyes. "What did you say?"

"She's lying to you. Ever since she destroyed our plans to merge with Fortescue, she's been desperate to get back into the board's good graces. This is her chance. She'll do anything to hand this hotel over to her father."

Because he wanted to punch Jerry right in his pretty face, Tony stuffed his hands in his pockets. "Is that why you made sure she was stranded in Tahiti?"

The anger in Jerry's eyes grew brighter. "I was doing us both a favor. You can't believe she really intends to marry you. She's going to string you along until she gets you to sign the hotel over to McNeil."

Tony's eyes narrowed. "Why are you telling me this?"

"Because I can get you a better deal. J.R. is desperate to get his hands on this place. So is my mother, for that matter."

"Why?" Tony asked, keeping his tone casual.

"Some deal she's worked out with someone in the mayor's office. They're going to turn the whole block into a huge hotel and conference center. I don't know all the details. The important thing for you to know is that acquiring this hotel is worth a lot of money to McNeil. I can promise you top dollar if you'll work with me."

"You're saying that Lily can't handle the deal?" Tony asked evenly.

"No. Of course not."

Something in his eyes must have warned Jerry because he continued in a milder tone. "I'm just saying that Lily is inexperienced. She's only been at the company for a little over a month. J.R. welcomed her back on March fifteenth and as a birthday present, he told her she could have the job of getting Henry's Place."

In spite of his attempt to hide it, Tony could hear both anger and frustration in Jerry's tone. Had Lily been the intended victim all along? Was he now looking into the eyes of a man who would hire someone to kill his stepsister?

LILY GLANCED AROUND the living room of the penthouse suite. Tony had led Jerry down into the sunken living room where Nick and Tyler had already drawn Pamela. Lucy and Grace were circulating with plates of hors d'ouevres, and Giles was talking to Gina on the patio. Everyone had been near the opened box of chocolates at least once.

In a moment, Gina would ask Giles to get her another glass of champagne. Lily drew in a deep breath and let it out. Though she couldn't have pointed to the exact moment, at some time during the brief scenes she'd played out with Giles, her father and Pamela, the nerves in her stomach had steeled into determination. The moment Giles stepped in from the patio, she moved quickly to join him at the bar.

Showtime.

"You're one of the few people here who seems to be having a good time," she commented.

"I like parties," Giles said as Vera tipped champagne into Gina's glass.

This was the trickiest part of the charade. Getting Giles to hand her the chocolate. The whole family had discussed various strategies. She could take one and drop it. Giles, the gentleman, would hand her another—though he'd likely hold out the box for her to choose one herself. She could pick up another flute of champagne and say that she was bringing it to Tony, and then ask Giles to select a piece of candy for her.

In the end, Lily found it easier to improvise. "I haven't had time to sample those chocolates yet. Why don't you pick one out for me? I have to keep my eye on Tony. I can tell by the way that muscle near his mouth is twitching that he's just about to punch Jerry in the face."

Giles chuckled as he chose a chocolate, then held it in front of her lips. Knowing that several pairs of eyes were on her, Lily took the candy into her mouth and chewed it carefully. As she did, she counted to ten. According to Drew, that was how long it would take a certain poison to work. As she swallowed, she quickly reviewed everything that Dame Vera had taught her. Then she widened her eyes and turned to Giles, reaching with one hand for his lapel. Her other hand went to her stomach as she coughed. Then she slid to the floor.

A.J. screamed right on cue. Pandemonium followed. Lily tried to keep track of the scene based on what she could hear. But it all seemed to happen at once.

Giles swore. That meant that Vera had spilled a drink on him to keep him occupied.

Glass shattered. That was Tyler's job.

Something heavy crashed—the coffee table. Sam had played his part.

"What happened? Let me through," Tony said.

Drew reached her first, just as they'd rehearsed. She felt two fingers press against her throat.

"Stand back," Drew said. "Give her room."

"I have to see her," Tony said. "What happened?"

"The candy," Dame Vera said. "He gave her a chocolate."

After all the noise, the sudden silence thundered in the room. Lily counted the beats off in her head. When she reached ten, Drew's fingers withdrew.

"I want to see her," Tony said.

Another three beats.

"No." Tony's voice was jagged with pain.

Another table fell. More glass shattered.

"Let me see her," Tony said.

Sounds of a scuffle followed. The way they'd rehearsed it, Sam and Nick were holding Tony back.

"Stand back," Drew said. "She's dead."

11

"DEAD? SHE CAN'T BE." Even as he registered shock and disbelief, Tony managed a quick look around the room. He knew his brothers and Nick were doing the same. Everyone was frozen in place. J.R. appeared to be stunned. Pamela's and Jerry's expressions were harder to read.

"She can't possibly be dead," Giles said. For the first time, Tony heard a trace of fear in the man's voice.

"I'll have to ask all of you to step down into the living area," Drew said, taking Giles's arm.

"No. You've made a mistake." Tony struggled to break free of the hold that Sam and Nick had taken on him. "Let me see her. She's just fainted."

Drew gripped Tony's shoulders and met his eyes. "She's dead."

"You're lying," Giles said. "What did she die of?"

"The chocolate," Dame Vera said in the voice that bounced off second balconies. She pointed a finger at Giles. "He poisoned her with chocolate."

"Poisoned," A.J. and Tyler echoed the word just as they'd rehearsed.

"No," Lucy said in a choked voice, reaching for her mother's hand.

"You bastard. You poisoned her." Breaking free, Tony lunged for Giles and grabbed him by the lapels of his coat.

"No," Giles managed to sputter as Tony's brothers pulled him away. He pulled out a handkerchief and wiped his forehead. "I have no reason to kill Lily."

"I want to see her." Tony struggled as Sam and Nick forced him down into the living room. "I have to see her."

"You can't." Drew urged an unresisting Giles onto a love seat. "I have to secure the crime scene. No one can go near her until the police arrive."

"Crime scene?" Coming out of his paralysis, J.R. spoke for the first time. "Who would want to kill Lily?"

"That's what I intend to find out." Drew met the eyes of each member of Lily's family as he pulled out his cell phone and punched in numbers.

Tony allowed Sam and Nick to push him into a chair. His job as the bereaved fiancé was to appear distraught. It was the most frustrating part of the whole charade and he'd argued against it. But his family had agreed that the scenario would be more credible if Drew handled the interrogation. Tony would have to be satisfied with grieving and gauging the reactions of the suspects.

"I've got a homicide to report." Drew spoke the words into his cell phone.

"No." Uttering the word as a moan, Tony slumped back into his chair and took another quick look around the room.

His family were playing their roles as if they'd been born for the stage. Gina had wrapped her arms around both of her daughters. Grace's face was white and Lucy was weeping silently into her mother's shoulder. Holding tight to Tyler's hand, A.J. wiped tears from her eyes.

His face white, J.R. sank into a chair. "No."

The best word Tony could come up with to describe Jerry's reaction was shell-shocked. But it was only mild annoyance that flickered over Pamela's face as she shifted her gaze to Giles. "You killed her?"

At the new accusation, Giles raised his hands, both palms outward. "Don't look at me. I had no reason to want her out of the picture."

"You handed her the chocolate," Drew pointed out.

"That box has been open on the bar for more than thirty minutes. Everyone in this room had access to it," Giles said.

"But you have motive. She dumped you two years ago, and your company stock took a hit—a bigger hit than McNeil Enterprises took," Drew said. "That couldn't have gone over well with your stockholders. And I imagine you assured them that nothing could possibly go wrong with the merger."

Giles shook his head. "That's water under the bridge. The stock recovered, and so did I. In fact, I prefer a bit of rivalry between the two companies. I think it makes us both sharper. Together, we might have become complacent and lost market shares." Giles shot a glance at Jerry. "Why don't you ask Jerry how he felt when the merger plans fell through?"

"Me?" Jerry sprang up from the chair he'd been sitting in.

"Jerry." Pamela spoke in a voice that rivaled Dame Vera's. It had the effect of putting her son right back in his chair.

A momma's boy, Tony thought, and one who had been furious when his stepsister had been taken back into the company. Maybe it was Jerry they should have "framed" for the poisoning.

"Jerry and Pamela were the ones who came to me with the plan for the marriage and the merger," Giles continued, "and they stood to make quite a bit of money on stocks and options once the merger went through."

Pamela's eyes narrowed. "We all did."

"Yes, but you would have gained the added advantage of getting Lily out of the company once and for all." Giles turned his gaze on Drew. "My job was to turn Lily into a little stay-at-home mom, thus clearing the way for Jerry to make an obstacle-free ascent up the corporate ladder to a vice presidency and eventually to the position of CEO."

"That's not true," Pamela said. "Jerry has a stellar future at McNeil Enterprises."

Giles's brows shot up. "Then why did Jerry find it necessary to have someone tamper with the company plane in Tahiti?"

"You bastard—"

Jerry's leap forward out of the chair was blocked when Sam stepped into his path and shoved him back into his seat.

"We were partners," Jerry said, glaring at Giles. "Delaying Lily's arrival was all your idea." He turned to the others. "I agreed to help keep Lily in Tahiti. That's all. Giles wanted to make his offer before she arrived at the hotel."

Giles sneered. "And you bungled even that."

J.R rounded on Jerry, a mix of fury and disbelief on his face. "You betrayed this company. You were actually working with Giles?"

"Yes," Jerry said, his jaw stiff with anger. "*Yes*, I betrayed your company, just as it betrayed me."

"Jerry." Pamela's voice was sharp.

"No, Mother, I'm going to tell him. Giles offered me a vice presidency if I could help him get Henry's Place. That was the position that I was guaranteed before the merger fell through."

"You fool." Pamela took a step toward her son, but J.R.'s hand on her arm stopped her.

"You could have had a vice presidency at McNeil," J.R. said. "It was just a matter of time."

"Too much time," Jerry said. "I've been working for ten years. And Lily comes back—the prodigal daughter returning—and you give her a job that I was supposed to have, a job that would have finally earned me the vice presidency you've been dangling under my nose for the past two years. If she'd been able to get the hotel for you, you'd have moved her right into a VP slot, and you'd have continued to stall me."

"So you killed Lily." Tony shot out of his chair and took two steps before his brothers grabbed him. This time he wasn't acting as he struggled to break free.

"No." Jerry threw up his hands as he cowered in his chair. "It wasn't me."

"Lily came back to the company and as a surprise birthday present, your stepfather gave her the job you believed was yours, and so you decided to get rid of her once and for all."

"No," Jerry said. "All I did was take a job with a rival company and make sure Lily was delayed in Tahiti. That's all. I swear it."

"You fool." Pamela's voice was shrill. "All you had to do was wait."

"Sit down." Sam spoke the words into Tony's ear. "Let Drew wrap this up."

It took all of Tony's control to clamp down on his fury as he allowed himself to be drawn back to his chair.

Pamela moved toward her son, but once more, J.R. stopped her. "Let him finish."

Jerry's face twisted into a sneer. "I figured I would eventually be welcomed back to the family with a vice presidency after I'd held that position for a while at Fortescue. But I didn't kill her." He pointed a finger at Giles. "There's the man with the motive. Ask him why he wanted this two-bit, fleabag hotel. He's the one who would have done anything to get it."

"Jerry's got a point," Drew said as he turned to Giles.

Giles raised his hands, palms out and said, "Ah, but I don't want the hotel as much as J.R. does. He's got a little revenge thing going, too. Henry Romano stole a woman away from him years ago." He shot a smile at his rival "We're a lot alike, J.R. Too bad the merger fell through."

All eyes turned toward J.R. His face was flushed, his eyes angry. "All right. I did vow revenge on Henry Romano when he convinced Isabelle Sheridan to break off our engagement. And when the opportunity to buy Henry's Place came up, I was only too happy to take it. But I wouldn't kill to get that revenge. I certainly wouldn't kill my own daughter. You on the other hand—"

Nick and Drew both blocked J.R. as he lunged toward Giles.

"You're knocking at the wrong door, J.R.," Giles

said. "If you want to know who hates your daughter enough to kill her, look in your own executive suite and ask yourself who's been hell-bent on keeping Lily out of it."

"Stop it!" Pamela screamed the words, and they stopped everyone in their tracks. There was fury in her eyes, ice in her voice. Every eye in the room was on her.

"You're fools, all three of you. You," she pointed her finger at Giles, "because you'd rather play little games of revenge than run your company. You," the finger shifted to J.R., "because you treat people so callously. If you'd just recognized Jerry's talent, his potential, he'd have had Henry's Place signed, sealed and delivered by now."

She was breathing hard, her hands were fisted, and there was nothing of the cool control that Tony had seen earlier.

"And you," she pointed her finger at Jerry, "You're a fool because you couldn't wait. You've always been too impatient. And now you've ruined everything. Another twenty-four hours, and I told you that I had everything arranged. We would have had everything. You just had to wait."

Pamela's voice had grown shriller as she spoke. Her face was red and her eyes were flashing. Everyone's gaze was fastened on her.

"What arrangements did you make?" Drew asked. "Did you hire another hit man?"

There was a beat of silence as Pamela turned toward him.

"You wanted both of them out of the way, didn't you?" Drew asked. "That way you would almost certainly get your hands on the hotel and you could tie up your deal with the city planning board, and Jerry would get the vice presidency you promised him two years ago."

"You don't know what you're talking about," Pamela said.

Tony saw that she was struggling for control. Then with some pride he watched Drew close in on her. "You were so close to everything you wanted two years ago. It must have been quite a setback when Lily canceled the wedding. All those stock options gone, Jerry whining that he wasn't being appreciated. And maybe J.R. held you responsible because you promoted the engagement and the merger. Then two years later, you've made amends by acquiring the real estate on this entire city block, which will make the acquisition of Henry's Place much more than revenge. It will restore the board's faith in you, and get your son the position you've promised him. Then comes the monkey wrench. On the fifteenth of March, Lily comes back on the scene and it's déjà vu. She's going to ruin everything again."

"You?" J.R. turned toward his wife. "You killed her?"

"No," Pamela said. "I didn't bring those chocolates. And no one in this room can say that I touched them."

"But you did hire a hit man," Drew said. "We've identified him, and he's been arrested. It's only a matter of time before he gives you up."

As Pamela's face whitened, Tony started to rise. Only the tightening of Sam's hand on his shoulder kept him in his chair.

"I don't think it will bother the jury that you didn't bring the chocolates," Drew continued, "or that no one caught you slipping a poisoned one into the box. I think they'll be more than happy to find you guilty.''

"I didn't kill her.'' Pamela's voice shook as she glanced around the room. Her husband and son were staring at her, their disbelief clear on their faces.

"And you've always called me callous,'' J.R. said as he stared at his wife.

Tony found himself staring at all three of the Mc-Neils. This was Lily's family. A father who hadn't shown any interest in going to his daughter even though he believed her dead, a stepbrother who hated her, and a stepmother who wanted her dead. Fury slapped into him so hard that he wasn't sure what he would have done if Lily hadn't chosen that moment to rise from the "dead.''

Fear replaced anger in a heartbeat as he watched her streak down the stairs. This wasn't part of the charade.

"No, you didn't kill me, Pamela.'' Lily pushed past her father to stand toe-to-toe with her stepmother. "But you did hire someone else to do the job for you.''

"You lying little cheat. You were just pretending.''

"Lily, what's the meaning of this?'' J.R. asked.

Tony rose and gripped J.R.'s arm. "Wait.'' Now that the first flash of fear had settled, he'd decided to play along with Lily's improvisation. Sam and Nick had moved so they were flanking Pamela. Drew was standing between Giles and Jerry. They had everyone guarded.

"Yes, I was pretending,'' Lily said. "This was all a little April Fools' joke, and it worked. It flushed out a would-be killer.''

Tony inched a little closer. So did Nick and Sam.

"All day today, I've been trying to picture first Giles

and then Jerry as killers. But neither of them has the passion. You do.''

"Lies," Pamela said. "You're making up lies."

"No. You tried to kill me. For the moment, we'll let that slide. The mistake you made was trying to kill Tony. That's unacceptable.''

Lily's fist came up and connected with Pamela's jaw. Hard. Nick and Sam caught her as she fell.

THE ROMANOS WERE EATING again. And talking all at once.

Total chaos, Lily thought as she let the shouted bits of conversation flow around her. A.J., Grace, and Nick were theorizing strategies that Pamela's defense lawyers would take, and then coming up with counter moves that the prosecution could make. Sam sat on the arm of A.J.'s chair, keeping his hand on her shoulder to prevent her from leaping up when the arguments heated up. Tyler was feeding her baby and supporting her husband's ideas each and every time he voiced one. Except for Drew who was pacing, his cell phone pressed to his ear, the rest of the family had formed a semi-circle around the lawyers, cheering one or the other of them on. Alistair and Vera had retired to the bar, celebrating the end of a case in true *Thin Man* fashion with martinis.

Lily sat on the couch in the middle of the noise and confusion, amazed that she was getting used to it. Not that she was joining them. She hadn't been able to eat a thing since that piece of chocolate. And she didn't have much to say. Any sense of relief that she felt watching Drew's men drag Pamela off had been tempered by the knowledge that a member of her own family had tried very hard to destroy Henry's Place and kill Tony. Then, to top it off, her father and Giles had lingered in an attempt to talk business with Tony.

When he'd refused to speak with either of them, they'd each taken her aside. Giles had merely taken her hand and repeated his offer of a job. That had, of course, infuriated her father who'd countered by assuring her that a vice presidency at McNeil Enterprises was hers if she could just bring the Romano hotel deal home. No goodbye. No hugs.

As she'd watched her father leave, she'd faced one reality head-on. No matter how she "visualized" him, her father was just not ever going to be the way she wanted him to be. The only person she could change was herself.

Her biggest concern right now was that Tony was angry. She could see it in the tensed muscles of his jaw and in the gestures he made, and whatever he was saying to Drew wasn't diffusing it.

Of course, he had every right to be angry. First of all, she hadn't followed the script. But surely, he could see that she couldn't just lie there and continue to play dead. She'd had a right to confront Pamela. There wasn't a doubt in anyone's mind that Pamela was guilty. She might not have confessed, but Sam had discovered that it was Pamela who had bought up the entire block surrounding the hotel, and she'd put McNeil Enterprises into a lot of debt doing it. Her deal with the city planners and, indeed, the very bright future she wanted for McNeil Enterprises, depended on McNeil getting hold of Henry's Place. The one thing she hadn't planned for was that Tony would refuse all offers.

Of course, Pamela had wanted her son to make the

deal, but barring that, she was prepared to do anything to ensure that the Romanos took the offer that McNeil was presenting. After all, if McNeil profited, so would she.

Lily could almost feel a bit sorry for the woman—and Jerry too. She'd never before realized that her father had treated them in the same cold and business-like manner that he'd always treated her.

One thing she knew for sure. She wasn't going back to McNeil Enterprises. Glancing down, she saw that she was gripping her hands together so tightly that her knuckles had turned white. Taking a deep breath, she drew her hands apart. The truth was she wasn't worried about her father or her next job. What was bothering her was the fact that deep down she knew that Tony was angry with her. He hadn't come near her since the police had dragged Pamela away.

"You'll feel better if you eat something," Dropping down on the couch beside her, Drew lifted a tray of stuffed mushrooms and offered it to her.

Lily stared at him. Those had to be the first words he'd ever spoken directly to her. "I can't eat right now."

He shrugged. "You'll have to work on it. Eating is how the Romanos get through every kind of crisis."

When she said nothing, he continued, "You have a nice right cross."

"Thanks."

"Look. I was wrong about you." He smiled then, and Lily saw that he had his own share of the Romano charm. "I hate it when that happens. Tyler and A.J. told me what you've done to save the hotel for Tony and for all of us." Then he held out his hand. "Welcome to the Romano family."

Lily's heart skipped a beat and then sank. Those were the words she wanted to hear from Tony.

Tyler chose that moment to hand her sleeping infant to Nick and raise her voice above the still-arguing lawyers. "Counselors and future counselors, I call for a brief recess. I have an announcement to make."

As if it were another well-rehearsed scene, Alistair and Vera set their martinis down and moved to pull down a movie screen on the upper level. Lucy raced up the two steps to the kitchen and rolled out a cart complete with a slide carousel.

"We're moving fast on this one," Drew said in a tone only Lily could hear. "Tyler decided a sneak attack would work best. Are you with us?"

"With you?" Lily asked.

Drew put a hand on her arm. "Shhh. She's going to present your plan to save the hotel. Just watch."

Lily did just that as the lights in the living room were turned off and the first slide lit up the screen. It was her plan all right—all mapped out with the modifications they'd discussed on the airplane. But Tyler had brought it to life. For ten minutes, there was only the sound of Tyler's voice explaining the flow charts and graphs. When the screen finally darkened and the lights in the room were turned on, Tony was frowning. Lily's stomach fluttered as silence lengthened in the room.

"This is Lily's idea, right?" Tony asked.

"Yes," Tyler said. "And the beauty of it is that it's so simple really. We form a family company, each of us invests according to our means, and you run the whole thing as CEO.''

"We're not taking no for an answer,'' Nick said. "We appreciate the job you've done running the hotel. But we all own a share of Henry's Place, so it's only fair that we all contribute to keeping it up and running.''

"We'll all get to share in the profits,'' Sam pointed out.

"And there *will* be profits,'' A.J. added. "Did you see Lily's projections?''

"Time to surrender gracefully, bro,'' Drew said.

Tony rose from his chair. "I need to speak with Lily. Privately.''

"Hey, if you're upset about this,'' Drew said, "take it out on us. All Lily did was come up with the idea. We're the ones who want to implement it.''

"It's all right.'' Lily had to push the words past the tightness in her throat. "I want to talk to Tony, too.'' Not that she was going to be given a choice since Tony already had her hand and was pulling her toward the bedroom.

As he closed the door, she moved to the bed and then turned to face him. He was pacing, his shoulders and jaw tensed, his hands fisted at his sides. She'd never seen him this angry.

"There's something I have to say.''

His words sounded a death knell in her ears. Had he dragged her in here to dump her? She couldn't feel her knees anymore, but she managed to climb up the steps to sit on the bed. Everything had started here. It might as well end here.

"It's... it's not going to work.'' Tony dragged a hand through his hair.

Lily's chin lifted. "I guarantee that what Tyler just outlined will work."

He waved a hand. "Of course it will. I'm not talking about the damned hotel. I'm talking about us."

Lily pressed a hand to her stomach. He *was* going to dump her.

"Dammit!" The word exploded into the room. "I wanted to do this right. I wanted to find the right words."

Her gaze flew to his face. Fury crackled around him. And suddenly, she was angry too.

Rising to her knees on the mattress, she fisted her hands on her hips. "Now wait just a minute. I just saved your hotel. And your life."

When he opened his mouth, she raised a hand to stop him. "Maybe you don't have the right words, but I do. And you're going to let me finish. I saved your life, Romano. Twice. First when the shooter fired at you—and again tonight because Pamela wouldn't have stopped at killing just me. Okay, maybe I saved my own life, too. And your family helped a little. A couple of crack P.I.s and a police detective are nothing to sniff at. But it was my plan that flushed Pamela out."

"Lily, I—" Tony moved to the side of the bed.

This time she cut him off by poking a finger into his chest. "And you're angry at me. You have the nerve to be angry just because you can't find the right words to dump me?" She poked him again even as a look of complete stupefaction appeared on his face. "If you think that you can just toss me away like a piece of—"

Tony grabbed both of her hands. "You think I brought you in here to dump you?" The laugh started deep in his chest and filled the room.

She jerked one hand free and punched him then—one good left jab in the stomach. Surprise and delight filled his eyes before he grabbed her shoulders and pinned her beneath him on the bed.

"Get off," she managed to huff.

Tony just grinned at her. Oh, she was a fighter all right.

"Get off."

"Not until we clear a few things up. First, I'm not angry with you. I'm furious with your father. It was all I could do to keep my hands off of him. He's a stupid man not to value you. And I'm angry with myself. Because I have something to say to you, and I wanted everything to be perfect."

She stared at him, not struggling anymore.

He took a deep breath. "I came in here to ask you to keep that ring on your finger. I want the engagement to be real. From the moment we made love in this bed, I knew you were right for me." His chocolate-brown eyes, soft with tenderness, wandered over her face, then met her gaze. "I want you to share my life."

Lily couldn't have named all the feelings streaming through her. Except for one. For the first time in her life she felt as if she belonged.

"Marry me," Tony said. "I'm not letting you out of this bed until you say yes."

DAME VERA TOOK HER ear off the glass she had pressed to the bedroom door. Then she turned to the Romanos who were waiting eagerly for the news.

"There's going to be a wedding," she said quietly in her best soothsayer's voice.

Alistair shook his head. "Now you know where she gets all her predictions."

But the Romanos weren't paying attention to him. They were too busy giving each other high fives and hugs.

"You're next, Drew," A.J. said as she slapped his hand.

"No," Vera corrected. "Alistair and I will be next."

"Here. Here," Drew said in a relieved tone. "I'll drink to that."

"THERE'S A DOWNSIDE to being part of this family." Tony whispered the words as he nibbled at Lily's earlobe.

"And that would be?" Lily could feel her mind clouding already and his lips were barely brushing against her skin.

"No privacy. Can't you hear them out there?"

"Yes." Shifting her head, she whispered, "About the privacy. I have this plan."

Tony laughed. "I'll bet you do. And it'll probably work."

Placing her hands on the sides of his face, she met his eyes. "Seriously. What do you think of my plan for the hotel?"

"It's perfect," he said. "You remember that old Ben Franklin saying, *Early to bed, early to rise?*"

"Yes."

"Well, I think it was a smart move on my part to take you early to bed."

Her eyes narrowed. "The way I remember it, it was as much my idea as yours."

He grinned at her. "Okay. I'll share the credit. Either

way, I'd say it was a good move on both our parts. To-gether, we've found a way to make all the Romanos wealthy, but they're going to have to handle the healthy and wise part on their own. From now on, I in-tend to focus all my attention on you. I love you, Lily McNeil.''

Lily laughed as she drew Tony's mouth to hers. "I love you too, Tony Romano.''

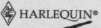

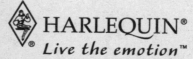

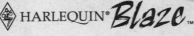

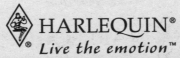

**Experience two super-sexy tales
from national bestselling author**

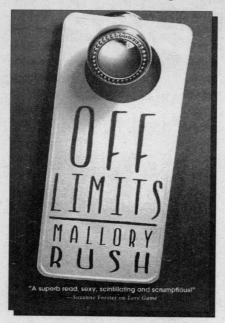

"A superb read, sexy, scintillating and scrumptious!"
—Suzanne Forster on *Love Game*

A collector's size volume
of HOT summer reading!

Two extraordinary women explore their deepest romantic desires
in Mallory's famously sensual novels, *Love Game* and *Love Play*.

Catch the sizzle…in May 2004!

"Ms. Rush provides an intense and outrageously sexy tale…"
—*Romantic Times*

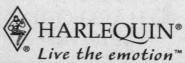

HARLEQUIN®
Live the emotion™

Visit us at www.eHarlequin.com

PHMR635

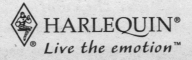

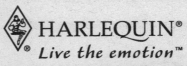